NEW YEAR IN PARADISE

DARCI BALOGH

Knowhere Media LLC

For Robert

My best friend and the love of my life.

Thank you for supporting me, believing in me, and for the countless cups of coffee and words of encouragement you have given me over the years. You have taught me what true love is.

I love you always.

ISBN 978-1-943990-33-7

Unattributed quotations are by Darci Balogh.

Cover designed by GetCovers

Chapter One

She stood waist deep in turquoise blue water. The tips of her fingers traced the surface as she moved her hands back and forth, back and forth, touching the ocean as if it were a fuzzy blanket.

The water was warmer than she expected it to be. Almost as warm as a bath, but not quite. Mellow waves, more like long bumps on the surface, pushed against her stomach rhythmically as they rolled past her towards the shore.

Without looking she knew the beach was white sand. Without looking she knew there was not another soul anywhere in sight. The gentle beauty of this place was for her and her alone, and that knowledge filled her with peace.

Flashes of bright orange, pink, and green, flitted through the water. Tropical fish, dozens of them, swam around her legs. She suddenly remembered that her feet were sunk into the ocean floor under the turquoise water. When she looked down she realized, for the first time, that she was fully clothed.

Her best business suit, her interview suit, crisp and ironed until it hit the water at her waist where the material, soaked through with salt water, floated languidly around her body.

Her heart quickened at the sight. This wasn't good. It would be ruined. She couldn't replace it in time for her interview. She would either have to go to the interview in a sopping wet business suit or go naked. Her heartbeat increased. Suddenly, she knew she was no longer alone.

Glancing to her left, then her right, just within her peripheral vision, she saw a sea of pink feathers looming. Flamingos. Hundreds of them. They made a beautiful cooing noise. Her heartbeat slowed. Calmer now. More brightly colored fish passed through the water in front of her. She knew what to do.

Bringing her hands up from her sides where they'd been tracing the surface of the ocean, she found the small business-like buttons that kept her stiff jacket closed and flicked them open until the jacket hung loose. Shrugging her shoulders, she slipped it off easily, letting it sink into the water at her back.

The cooing of the flamingos grew louder and she smiled, knowing they were encouraging her. Quickly, she unbuttoned her pale blue silk shirt that went so well with the grey of her interview suit. It, too, was taken by the ocean. Fed to the fish for all she cared.

Within a few moments, she was completely naked, standing proudly in the turquoise water, tropical fish brushing playfully against her legs, a mass of flamingos pressing her on from behind. Without another thought, she took a deep breath and dove head first into the water.

Rowan Murray woke with a start. Her eyes darted around in confusion.

Rowan, Ro for short, wasn't standing up to her waist in water. She was slumped uncomfortably in the middle seat on an airplane. Looking from side to side, she saw that she was not flanked by hoards of pink cooing flamingos. Rather by oversized tourists, stuffed first into their khaki shorts and bright colored T-shirts, then into their seats, and finally strapped tightly with their seatbelts.

On her right was a thick middle-aged man with extra wide shoulders that took up all of the room across the back of his seat as well as some of the room behind her. On her left was an even thicker middle-aged woman. The woman had the window seat. She, too, was running out of room in her assigned area and spilling over into Ro's narrow middle seat.

Ro sucked in her breath and looked down at her own form taking up the little room remaining between the larger than life couple on her left and right. Thankfully, she wasn't naked. She'd been dreaming. Ro had a twinge of disappointment when she realized that she had not been swimming with tropical fish in a turquoise ocean. At least, not yet.

"Dozed off, did ya?" the man asked with an enthusiastic smile.

Ro nodded. She pulled herself back into a sitting position, which wasn't easy given the limited amount of room.

"Well, you weren't snoring at least," he continued, laughing out loud at the thought of it.

He may not have been sleeping, but he'd certainly been drinking. Ro instinctively leaned towards the woman. She may suffocate in the pillow of her bosom, but she'd rather do that then have to fend off any clumsy advances from an overly friendly seat-mate, accidental or otherwise.

Slipping her phone out of the front pocket of her short black cotton dress, Ro checked the time. Less than an hour until they landed. Less than 24 hours until her scheduled interview.

"The captain said we're landing early," the woman told her, a smile lighting up her fleshy face. She nudged Ro, nearly knocking her into the intruding shoulder and bicep of her other neighbor, "You're anxious to get on with your vacation, aren't you?"

"Actually, I'm interviewing for a job. I'm moving here," as the words came out of her mouth, Ro still could hardly believe it was true.

"Moving to Playa del Carmen?" The woman, apparently, was blown away by the idea.

"Really?" Mr. Big Shoulders chimed in.

Ro nodded, "Really."

"You're American?" the woman asked.

Ro wasn't sure why that made a difference, but she nodded again as she answered, "Yes, I'm from Indiana."

"How did you decide to move to someplace like that?" the woman asked, still a little dumbfounded at the concept.

How indeed.

The idea had come to her only eight weeks ago, the Monday after her 31st birthday. But Ro knew the motivation behind it had begun over two years earlier.

That was when she'd broken up with her fiancé. Well, he'd broken up with her. Actually, he'd cheated on her with her friend and they'd had a huge fight where they broke up with each other. But, whatever. The end result was that they broke up and she moved on, mostly.

Theo. That was his name.

After the initial anguish of the betrayal had worn off, Theo had insisted they remain friends. And Ro, being a modern kind of girl, had agreed to stay connected on Instagram and every other social media platform they were connected.

Initially, watching Theo have fun without her was incredibly painful. She coped with it a little better when he went on what appeared to be long drinking binges full of meaningless one-night stands instead of dating one single girl. At least he wasn't marrying any of them.

That fact kept Ro sane as she created a life after Theo. Slowly their awkward friendship drifted into the realm of social media and occasional meetings at a mutual friend's party, nothing more.

All had been well and Ro thought she'd truly moved on, until just after Christmas last year.

An image of Theo with a blue-eyed blonde popped up on his Instagram. It looked like they were at a bar and it looked like they were having fun. A lot of fun. For the next few months the blonde kept showing up more and more frequently. Ro couldn't keep from watching.

That was the thing about social media. It was a great way to keep in touch and stay connected. But some things, perhaps, were better left disconnected.

Ro knew with everything in her soul that there was something different about this blonde, something more in Theo's expression when they were cheek to cheek in a selfie. Ro knew because she had experienced first hand what Theo looked like when he was falling in love. He used to look at her the way he looked at the blue eyed blonde.

Tamara was her name.

Being the modern, independent, ex-fiancé who had moved on with her life, Ro handled the situation like a pro. She online stalked Theo and Tamara relentlessly. Daily. Hourly even.

Winston, her friend from work, said she needed to delete Theo from all of her social media and her phone. Or, instead of deleting his phone number, rename him in her cell as "Jerk Who Slept With My Friend" or "Liar Who Asked Me To Marry Him Then Cheated", or something of that nature. She knew he was right, but Ro couldn't bring herself to do it. She was addicted to watching Theo and Tamara's relationship. Salaciously drinking in every perfect moment they shared.

Ro watched as they fed each other sushi in New York, as

Theo taught Tamara how to snowboard in Colorado, and when Tamara surprised Theo with the newest iPhone on his birthday. Their engagement, not even a year after meeting, threw Ro into a pity party of epic proportions. Still, she couldn't stop following their love story. The love story that was supposed to be hers.

"They're not as happy as they look," Winston had told her for the thousandth time. "Guys like that don't change. He didn't change for her, she's just willing to put up with his bull-shit so she can look happy on Instagram."

He had walked into her tiny office and found her sunk in her chair staring at her phone, looking dejected. Moving some papers aside, he placed the hazelnut latte he brought her every morning on her desk.

"I know," Ro groaned.

She did know, yet her thumb kept scrolling through the images of Theo getting on one knee, of the pale blue Tiffany ring box, of the horse drawn carriage he'd arranged to carry them away, of the hundreds of congratulatory comments.

"Maybe you should take a vacation," Winston suggested. He nodded towards the phone in her hand. "From that thing for sure."

He plopped down in the chair on the other side of her desk, taking a sip of his coffee. His suit was a good cut and he wore it casually. A good looking guy, medium height, brown hair, brown eyes, Winston called himself the 'poster boy for average'. But he was cool, as accountants go anyway.

Ro put her phone face down on her desk and picked up her drink. "There. Done."

"Good, now book a cruise or something," Winston teased.

"You're one to talk," Ro answered, grinning at him. "When was the last time you took a vacation, exactly?" It was a rhetorical question. They both knew Winston had never taken a vacation.

She and Winston had started working for Strathum Inc. on the same day. They attended all of the on boarding Human Resources orientations together, and even filled out their health insurance and 401K forms while sitting next to one another.

Winston was an accountant and Ro was an administrative assistant for the accounting department. They'd been at Strathum for over five years. In that time Winston had only used two weeks of his vacation time to help his aging parents move into a condo, one week for his Grandmother's funeral, and two days to attend his brother's wedding in California.

"What can I say, I love my job," Winston said. He leaned back in his chair and put his feet up on her desk as if to show the level of his satisfaction.

Ro looked around her small office, the multiple large framed posters of flowers, a sign that read "Welcome to the Accounting Department, Where Everybody Counts" and her house plants thriving where they were perched on top of the file cabinets. Windowless, yet cheery, she'd moved into this office three years before when Cynthia had retired and Ro had taken her place.

Now it seemed to Ro that she'd been in that little office her entire life. Watching other people get what they wanted while her dreams always fell short. Always ending unsatisfactorily. She had just turned 31, and this was her life?

Ro sighed, "I need more than a vacation from this place. I need a vacation from my life."

And that's when the first nugget of an idea formed in her mind. The tiny spark of inspiration to change her life in a sweeping way started during that conversation with Winston. Every time she saw a new post from Theo where he and Tamara were taste testing wedding cakes or planning their exotic honeymoon in Bali, she was spurred on to look for a way to upgrade her own life into one that was exciting and worthy to show off on social media.

That initial spark had ended with her sandwiched between the two large tourists on her way to interview as a secretary to Cooper Rivera, owner of the Hotel Diamante in Playa del Carmen, Mexico. Just three days before New Year's Eve.

Her New Year resolution this year was to have a wild and adventurous life. Period.

Ro's phone buzzed and she looked down to see a text message from Winston.

It's quiet here without you. Let me know when you land.

She smiled. Winston had taken her to the airport to see her off. He was the only person she would miss terribly, but she had to do what she had to do. He had moped about it for weeks, but in the end Winston was a good friend and he understood.

A dinging sound rang through the cabin and the flight attendant's voice came over the speakers, asking them to turn off their electronic devices and buckle their seatbelts. The plane would be landing soon.

Ro followed the instructions. If she craned her neck just a little, she was able to look around the form of the woman at the window seat and see a sliver of bright sun and blue sky. She knew Palm trees, white sand beaches and a turquoise blue ocean were somewhere below them. Maybe even Flamingos.

Ro felt a thrill of possibility rush through her. Something she hadn't felt in a very long time.

With any luck she would impress Mr. Rivera, land the job, and be ringing in the new year with a brand new life.

Chapter Two

Ro stepped out of the cab in front of the Hotel Diamante at 8:30 am, 30 minutes before her scheduled interview. Shocked that she was on time at all after the morning she'd had, she paid the cab driver their previously agreed upon 75 Pesos, fumbling with the unfamiliar currency. The driver took the money, grunted his thanks in Spanish and made a U-turn in the narrow street to head back to the busier section of town. She watched the small, beat up cab retreat, then took a deep breath and turned her attention to the front of the Hotel Diamante.

The three-story hotel had a Spanish colonial style charm. Clay tile steps led up from the street into a courtyard. Beautiful blue and white tile work surrounded a crystal blue rectangular shaped fountain that shot water nearly as high as the third story before it fell in fat drops back into the water below. The falling water made a pleasing sound, almost like rain. Both sides of the courtyard had second and third story iron balconies, which all boasted glass French doors at the back, presumably leading to hotel suites.

Ro smoothed the front of her bright yellow sundress. She

had started off the morning in her lucky interview outfit, the sleek, grey business suit with the narrow skirt, lined jacket, and pale blue silk shirt she had worn in her dream. However, she hadn't made it out of the lobby of her hotel before realizing that the deeply unforgiving humidity was not going to allow her to wear her good luck clothes. Droplets of sweat rolled down her sides and back and she dared not take off the jacket until she was back in her room because the pale blue silk was splotched with giant patches wet from her sweat.

In a panic, Ro had gone through all of her most appropriate second choices, most of which came up unsatisfactory. She'd finally chosen the yellow sundress, even though it looked a bit too cheery for a job interview. Still, it was cotton, it went past her knees and it wasn't too low cut. Getting a job using her cleavage, as minimal as it might be compared to some, wasn't her style. She dug out her lightweight, white shell sweater that she put on to cover her shoulders. The result was passable. Not her lucky interview suit, but it would do. Maybe she needed a new kind of luck here in Playa del Carmen anyway.

Ro took a deep breath and said quietly, "No time like the present."

She walked past the crystal fountain up the three tiled steps to the front doors. Old, heavy wood frames with thick beveled glass from top to bottom, she took hold of the wide iron handle and pulled. Opening the door to her future.

A cool breeze rushed past her as she stepped into the lobby. A mixture of air-conditioning and fans, she thought, thankful for the relief from the oppressing humidity outside. The square clay tiles from the courtyard were continued into the lobby, except these tiles were twice as large. The lobby walls reached up the full three stories of the building, topped off by skillfully carved wooden beams that supported a domed, glass ceiling. A grand staircase curved up from her left, the heavy wooden banister looked antique and matched the beams in the glass ceiling. Elevator doors were on her right and located dead center underneath the glass ceiling was the front desk decorated with elegant mosaic tiles.

Behind the desk stood a man of about 30, short with the dark complexion and thick black hair of the area. He wore a crisp off white, short-sleeved shirt with gold buttons and a gold nameplate that said 'Carlos'. Behind Carlos were three double sets of French doors.

"Buenos dias, Señorita," said Carlos, smiling broadly at her with large white teeth.

"Buenos dias," Ro responded. Her nerves were tumbling through her stomach. She'd studied Spanish in high school and was pretty good at enunciation for ordering in restaurants, but that was about it. Over the past few weeks she'd gotten the most basic Spanish phrases memorized. Right now, she really hoped Carlos spoke at least a little English. "I'm Rowan Murray, I have a meeting with Mr. Rivera today."

Without missing a beat, Carlos moved into broken, but completely passible, English and Ro breathed a sigh of relief. Of course, she would learn the language if she got the job. For now, however, she silently blessed Carlos for his ability to communicate.

"Señor Rivera? Of course, you sit, please. I am getting him for you," Carlos said.

There were two Victorian style love seats placed against opposite walls under large potted palms. Ro walked to them to wait, but did not sit down. She was too nervous to sit down. She was about to meet Cooper Rivera, jet setting millionaire, owner of this hotel and, hopefully, her soon-to-be boss.

She'd Googled Cooper before accepting this interview. Her mother had insisted, though Ro would have done it without her mother's advice. Flying to another country to meet a man you'd only spoken to via emails to interview for a fantasy job could be considered a dream come true. Not double-checking his credentials, however, would have gone against Ro's cautious nature.

"What'd you find out about dream boss?" Winston had asked her after she told him about the job interview and that she was planning to do some online digging. Winston, like her mother, was anxious about her big life change. Though he was trying to be more supportive and laid back about it than her parents.

"Let's see, I found pictures and videos of him with friends, partying in Italy, on yachts, at charity balls. In those pictures he was usually with his father. I actually found out more about his Dad than him," she answered.

"What'd you find out about his Dad?" Winston sipped his coffee as he leaned back in the chair across from her desk. His daily ritual unchanged even as she was about to shift her entire existence.

"His Dad is a well known business man, millionaire type. He owns a lot of companies and is based in Arizona. He also owns a lot of property in Central and South America, plus a few interests in Europe. Big in a few charities. A few articles written about him online. He's mentioned once in a Forbes article."

Winston's eyebrows lifted in surprise at the mention of Forbes. Then he asked, "So, no prison sentences? No ugly lawsuits? No history of kidnapping beautiful women and selling them into the black market?"

Ro laughed, "No, not that I could find."

What she did find, but didn't tell Winston, was that Cooper Rivera was a very attractive man. Dark, chiseled, black hair, square jaw, full lips, and in all of the pictures she found he was wearing either a tuxedo or a swimsuit. In a few pictures he was wearing his tuxedo shirt untucked and only partly buttoned, his bow tie loose and hung around his neck. Those images popped into her mind as she waited in the lobby of his hotel and her stomach flipped with nerves.

Ro wouldn't say she was particularly beautiful. About 5'7", brown hair cut just below her chin, what one might call a cute, heart shaped face, and a nice wide smile. She did have a slim figure and was reasonably sure that she could turn a few heads on a good day.

Her eyes were probably her most arresting feature. Coming from a multi-ethnic ancestry ranging from Scottish to Italian to Indian, her great-grandmother was from India, Ro's skin had always been a uniquely golden brown. Her blue-grey eyes were that much more noticeable because of her skin tone. But she wasn't sure an astonishingly good looking and wealthy man would be terribly interested in her eyes.

She shook her head, silently admonishing herself for letting her mind slip into the fantasy that this meeting was anything more than an interview. Cooper Rivera had never seen her and, as far as he knew, she had never seen him. This whole move to create a new life for herself was not about finding a man, it was about living an exciting and adventurous life. The kind of life she had thought she was going to have with Theo.

Theo was tall, dark and handsome. She rolled her eyes at the thought. Maybe she had a weak spot for that kind of guy.

"Miss Murray?" A woman's voice came from behind.

Ro turned quickly to see an older Mexican woman. She was thick bodied and sharply dressed, with black-rimmed glasses and dark red lipstick applied expertly to her full lips.

"Yes, I'm Rowan Murray."

The older woman stuck out her manicured hand. "I'm Alicia Perez, the GM of the Hotel Diamante. You're early."

Ro couldn't tell if this was a positive or negative statement, or merely an observance of the facts. She loved how the woman said 'Hotel Diamante', as if she were announcing it over the radio on a commercial.

"Yes, I wasn't sure how long it would take to get here," Ro answered.

"You didn't stay here?" Alicia Perez scowled at this realization. Carlos had returned to his position behind the desk and he glanced nervously at Ro, as if to say 'you should have stayed here'.

"No, I didn't," Ro admitted.

She had thought it might be uncomfortable or strange to stay at this hotel if the interview didn't go well, so had booked a modest room nearby. Suddenly, she was worried that her chances of getting the job may be affected by this decision.

Alicia extended her manicured hand across the desk towards Carlos, who started slightly as if her arm was a snake lunging at him. Alicia didn't look at him as she spoke.

"12-B," she said curtly. Her palm faced up and she motioned towards Carlos with her fingers, her rings clicking against the counter top as her fingers flicked back and forth.

Carlos quickly grabbed a key card, typed something into the slim laptop that sat on the counter, swiped the card through a machine and handed it to Alicia. As Carlos worked efficiently behind her, Alicia gazed steadily at Ro, who found it impossible to return the stare. She glanced away twice, once when the French doors behind the counter opened, revealing a long hallway that ended in what looked like a luxurious swimming pool in another courtyard, and once when she simply looked at her own feet.

"Now you stay here," Alicia said with finality, handing Ro the card Carlos gave her.

"Thank you," Ro answered.

"We will send for your things," Alicia shot a look to

Carlos who nodded in agreement. "Where did you stay last night?"

"The Palma Grande," Ro answered.

Alicia grimaced and made a tsk-tsk noise with her mouth. Carlos picked up a wafer thin phone and started dialing. Alicia started towards the staircase that Ro had passed on the way in.

"Come with me, I will show you to your desk," Alicia said.

"My desk?"

Alicia continued walking and Ro followed. She gave a backwards glance to Carlos, who she felt was the only person that might understand her confusion. He was speaking Spanish so fast into the phone she couldn't even recognize any of the words, but he managed to give her an encouraging smile and a thumbs up.

Alicia's high heels clicked confidently on the clay tile as she walked. Ro hurried to catch up.

"I think there may be a mistake. I don't think I have a desk. I'm here for an interview with Mr. Rivera?" The last few words came out as a question.

"There is no mistake," Alicia said. She paused at the foot of the stairs and looked back at Ro. "You're hired."

Despite her desire to remain professional, Ro's mouth dropped open. She watched Alicia climb the stairs, her high heels silent now as she was putting all of her weight on her toes. Realizing that she was falling behind, the younger woman had to hurry again to catch up.

"I'm hired?" Ro asked at the top of the stairs, slightly out of breath from rushing.

Alicia looked at Ro sideways as they moved together along a catwalk that overlooked the lobby below, "Yes, your terms of employment are on your desk ready for you to review. If you find them satisfactory, you will sign the paperwork and begin working today." She said the words with perfect pronunciation. Still, Ro was confused.

"I don't understand, I thought I was going to *interview* today."

Alicia stopped suddenly and faced Ro. "Your references are outstanding. Your resume impeccable. Do you want to work for the Hotel Diamante as an administrative assistant?"

"Yes," Ro answered.

"Interview completed. You're hired." Alicia whisked her hand once across the front of her face like she was shooing away a fly. "Here is your desk." She turned on her heel and opened a door on the wall behind them. Ro followed her into a beautiful space.

The room was full of light. It was painted in a creamy cocoa with white trim. There were high ceilings, iron lanterns for hanging lights and several tall windows with natural wood blinds along the outside wall. The clay tiles outside the room were replaced with mosaic tiles in rich browns and blues, which had been laid so they looked like a huge rug covering the floor. The first section of the room had a loveseat and two chairs that were cousins to the Victorian love seats in the lobby. A large impressionistic style painting of an open-air market hung above the loveseat.

A wide arched doorway led into the second section of the room with the same elegant windows along the outside wall. A slender polished wood desk sat facing the windows, its back to another arched doorway that was a double door. Both doors were closed. There were floor to ceiling bookshelves along the back wall full of hardback gold embossed books and shining knickknacks.

On the surface of the desk there was only a slim laptop and phone like what she'd seen Carlos use, a thin lamp with a shade made to look like a sepia toned map, a decorative piece of white coral, and a small white vase full of pink flowers.

There was also a single piece of cream colored Hotel Diamante stationary. She assumed this was the job offer information.

"Sit here and read through the details," Alicia instructed her as she swept her hand towards the paisley upholstered rolling chair behind the desk. "I will return shortly and you may give me your decision then."

Ro went to the chair to do as she was told. Alicia turned to leave.

"Excuse me," Ro said.

Alicia turned back.

"Do you know when I will meet Mr. Rivera?" She was, after all, going to be his administrative assistant.

A flash of annoyance crossed Alicia's face and came out in her tone, "Mr. Rivera is unavailable at present." Her eyes flicked to the double doors behind Ro, then back. "When he does emerge, it will be through those doors behind you."

Ro turned to look at the heavy, closed doors. Surprised, she asked, "This is where he lives?"

"Those doors lead to his office. At the back of his office is the entry to his suite. And, yes, he does live here." Alicia gave her a sharp look. "This is his hotel, after all."

With that comment, Alicia was gone.

Ro looked around the gorgeous little office space and let out her breath. She picked up the paper and tried to read it, but her mind was spinning. She couldn't focus. She stood up and went to the window, peering through the wooden blinds at the view. This side of the building didn't face the ocean, but it did overlook the vibrant street and town beyond.

Old buildings in a similar style to the hotel were packed close together. Climbing plants stretched from the ground up and over the buildings, bursting with bright red and pink flowers. Small cars maneuvered erratically through the street and Ro thought she could see the edge of an open market that continued out of sight. She wondered if it was the same open market in the painting.

Returning to the desk she sat down with intent and picked up the paper. Scanning it quickly, it seemed like an honest and generous offer, considering her cost of living would be less here than it was in America. The nerves in her stomach became a tingling excitement that filled her whole body. She put the paper back on the desk and noticed that her fingers were trembling.

Ro knew what she was going to do. The thrill of it was difficult to contain. She rummaged through her purse and pulled out her cell phone. It wasn't yet 9:00 am. Quickly, because she wanted to read through the offer details thoroughly before signing them, Ro typed a text to Winston.

I got the job!!!

She slipped the phone back into her purse, not waiting for his reply.

Chapter Three

After reviewing the job details more carefully, Ro had no reservations about signing her name on the dotted line. It wasn't a contract, per se, simply an offer of pay, which was nominal, but it did include a room at the hotel and three meals a day at the hotel restaurant, which made up the difference. The duties listed included answering the phone, scheduling Mr. Rivera's meetings and daily affairs as well as trips, filing, reviewing his expense accounts and making necessary payments, and email duties as assigned by Mr. Rivera. Pretty basic administrative stuff. Ro signed her name with a flourish to accept the terms of employment and sat back in her new chair.

She took a few moments to enjoy her new surroundings, running her hand along the polished surface of her lovely new desk, and leaning in to gaze at the white coral. She thought it might be a good idea to familiarize herself with her new office.

Getting up she looked over the decorative items on the bookshelves then opened the small cabinets that were along the bottom of each one. Inside there was what looked like a narrow printer/scanner combination, probably operated on wi-fi. There were also paper supplies, pens, highlighters, a stapler, your standard office fare. The sight of them in this luxurious and exotic location surprised her. She'd expected something different. Something more magical than an open box of neon yellow highlighters.

A series of three thumps coming from the other side of the closed double doors startled her. She stood like a deer in headlights, not blinking, not moving. Listening.

There they were again. Muffled thumps. Three in rapid succession. Then nothing. The ambient sound of the room buzzed in Ro's ears. Her heartbeat quickened.

The front door of the office pushed open and Ro jumped at the sound. She'd been focusing all of her attention on the double doors to the mysterious Mr. Rivera's office.

Alicia stepped in the door and towards Ro's desk, eyeing the signed paper, her high heels clicking neatly on the tile floor.

"You have accepted the terms?"

Ro nodded, glancing once away from Alicia to the double doors. No more sounds emerged.

Alicia picked up the paper and skimmed over it. When her eyes came to Ro's signature, she smiled. Ro found that she was surprised to see the older woman smile and even more surprised at the warmth behind it. There were crow's feet wrinkles at the corners of Alicia's eyes.

"Good, I will send Gloria to set up your passwords and answer your questions," Alicia said. She noticed Ro wrinkling her brow and anticipated her question. "Gloria is my administrative assistant. She knows everything there is to know about this job."

"Oh, I see," Ro said. She was to be solely Mr. Rivera's assistant. Somehow, after the thumping, she was a little apprehensive about it.

"Carlos will show you your room as well. He should have your things moved there by lunch. You will join me in the restaurant for lunch?" Although it was framed as a question, Ro didn't think she actually had a choice. She nodded.

"Excellent."

And that it was.

Gloria, a grey haired, round faced woman with impeccable English, joined Ro soon after Alicia excused herself. Gloria wore a feminine below the knee floral print dress and may have been four feet tall if she stood up straight, which she no longer could because of the bending of age. Where Alicia looked high-powered corporate, Gloria looked like she could out type, out bake and out knit anyone for miles.

Not only did she speak perfect English, but to Ro's surprise, the elderly lady was wicked fast on the computer. Within half an hour Ro had been added to the hotel's operating software, which seemed to be state of the art. Ro had a moment of concern when she realized that she had no training in the software program. Gloria patted her hand kindly.

"This is for reservations and inventory, which is usually what I work on with Alicia," Gloria reassured her. "You will work mostly with Cooper using Google calendar and email...and text," here the old lady sighed quietly, "He loves text."

Gloria gave Ro basic information on the hotel. When it was first built, the 19th century. When it became a hotel, 1998. And when Cooper Rivera purchased it, just two years earlier.

"Some say he acquired it in a poker game," Gloria said. Her old, dark eyes twinkled with humor, "But I don't think he's that good at poker."

Ro laughed, then asked, "So how do you think he acquired it?"

Gloria glanced at the double doors, ensuring they were closed before answering, "I think his father bought it for him. And I think his father expects him to use it...wisely."

"I see," Ro said, although she didn't. Not exactly.

"Knock knock," Carlos said as he opened the front door and entered. Bowing slightly in their direction he lifted his gaze to Ro and she could see the smile in his eyes. "May I show you to your quarters?"

She smiled, "Of course, thank you."

Her quarters were a large bedroom with a small balcony overlooking the courtyard that contained the swimming pool. The same brown and blue mosaic tiles that graced the floors elsewhere in the hotel were lain in a rug pattern on her bedroom floor and in the gorgeous bathroom. The deep luxury bathtub and separate shower were the nicest she'd ever seen, let alone used. A large mirror framed in dark wood that matched the vanity was framed with black iron lamps covered in creamy white shades.

She had just a few minutes to put away some of her things in the antique dark wood dresser that graced the wall opposite her Queen sized bed. The bed had more pillows than Ro would need stacked three deep against a fabric headboard upholstered in a deep mustard yellow. There was a small table with two sitting chairs in the corner of the room and a flat screen TV hanging on the wall above the dresser. Ro took her toiletries into the bathroom and freshened up for her lunch with Alicia. Perhaps Mr. Rivera would finally make his appearance when they were eating together.

No such luck.

Lunch was amazing, chilled cantaloupe soup followed by spicy garlic shrimp. The dining area was even more beautiful than the lobby, if that was possible. The tables were located on a wide, covered terrace that dripped with overgrown climbing plants covered in flowers. Each table was placed to provide an unobstructed view of the beach and ocean in the near distance. As Ro entered to meet Alicia, a warm breeze carried the fresh, salty scent of the sea and mingled with the delicious smells of the kitchen.

She was almost shocked to see the glistening blue of the ocean water. Her interview and hiring had monopolized her attention since she landed yesterday. She promised herself that the first moment she had alone, she would go to the beach and soak it all in.

That moment, however, would have to wait.

"Our focus right now needs to be 100% on the New Year's Eve party," Alicia told Ro, Gloria and Carlos. Apparently they were the dream team of the Hotel Diamante. Ro was excited about this, and more than a little apprehensive.

"I have the updated list of all of the vendors who will be here between now and 3:00 pm on the 31st," Gloria pulled neatly printed sheets out of nowhere and handed them each a copy. She said something quickly to Carlos in Spanish. He smiled and nodded.

Ro scanned the sheet and her heart filled with dismay. It was in Spanish. They must have assumed she was bi-lingual when she applied. She couldn't blame them, it would have been a natural assumption. Her stomach sank knowing that she couldn't take this job after all.

"I'm sorry, I don't speak Spanish," Ro said, glancing apologetically at Alicia. "Not yet, anyway. I was planning on learning," she added quickly. "But I think, maybe, you need someone who is bi-lingual for this position?"

"Oh, my apologies," Gloria said sweetly, pulling another piece of paper from somewhere and placing it in front of Ro. The names of the vendors were still in Spanish, of course, but the categories, assignments and notes were all in English.

Relieved, but still uncertain, Ro felt heat fill her cheeks. She didn't want to be a burden. It was foolish of her to expect special treatment just because she'd never taken the time to learn more than one language.

Alicia seemed to understand the issue and leaned forward, "Mr. Rivera does not speak Spanish. It was not a requirement for your position." She peered at Ro over her reading glasses, "Although, if you chose to learn the language it would only be beneficial."

Ro was surprised at how high her heart soared at this statement. She almost laughed out loud with relief. The disappointment she'd felt at the possibility of losing this job she'd had for only a few hours was intense. She made a mental note to get the latest and best language teaching software as soon as possible. Then, gaining control of her sudden elation, she looked down and studied her schedule intently.

The New Year's Eve celebration was a huge event, Alicia explained. And it was one that the Hotel Diamante had become famous for throwing without a hitch. Since Ro was brand new, Alicia would leave her in the capable hands of Gloria to do whatever might be most helpful. Carlos would take charge of his duties on the list, and Alicia would be checking in with everyone periodically for updates.

With the business taken care of, and their plates empty, Alicia excused herself to return to her office.

"Take a full hour for your lunch," she commanded as she stood. "The next few days will be incredibly busy, you may not have another chance to relax."

Alone at last, Carlos and Gloria turned their attention towards Ro, welcoming her warmly to the hotel as their co-worker.

"How is your room?" Carlos asked gallantly, his broken English more and more charming the longer Ro listened to him.

"It's really beautiful," she said, gushing a little bit.

Carlos' smile grew wider, revealing even more of his large, white teeth, "Bien, bien!"

"Have you been to visit the beach since you arrived?" Gloria asked.

"No, I haven't. I mean to. It's been a bit of a whirlwind," Ro responded.

"No beach?" Carlos was astonished.

"I will. I just haven't had time," she tried to reassure him.

"The beach is lovely in the morning," Gloria said, her eyes dreamy.

"I'm sure," Ro said, trying to be as agreeable as possible.

After lunch Ro returned to her post in front of the still closed double doors. Gloria had given her a few small things to do for the party, but assured her that Cooper would be making an appearance soon and she would have plenty to keep her busy.

It was funny how Gloria called him Cooper when everyone else referred to him as Mr. Rivera. Ro wondered if it had something to do with age. Gloria was quite a bit older than all of them, perhaps that meant she only had to use first names. Being in a different culture left a lot of questions open. Ro didn't know the ins and outs of social niceties in the Yucatán Peninsula. Maybe they were very different than Indiana. Well, she would just have to be as polite as she knew how to be, learn the language, and hope that she didn't make any major screw ups.

She was pondering these issues with so much concentration, that she didn't hear the door handle on the double doors click and turn. Nor did she hear the swish of the large doors pulling open across the smooth, tile floor. What she did notice was a draft of cool air coming from behind her, tickling the backs of her arms.

Ro turned her head to see where the draft was coming from and cried out, "Oh my God!" She jumped up from her chair and whirled around, sending her chair shooting backwards, directly into the man standing in the open doorway.

He made an 'oof' sound as the chair hit his abdomen.

Ro's hands flew up and covered her mouth, which was still gaping open. Heart pounding, she tried to regain her composure. The man in the doorway was well over six feet tall, short, black hair, dark complexion, chiseled features, with a well built, athletic body. She knew this because he wore a pair of slim fitted swim shorts in navy blue, and that was all. It was like the swimsuit that Daniel Craig made famous in James Bond, trim, tailored, not leaving a lot to the imagination.

It was Cooper Rivera. She recognized him immediately from her online stalking. Jet setting playboy. Son of a multimillionaire. Owner of this hotel. Her new boss.

She dropped her hands from her mouth, "I am so sorry."

"I didn't know anyone was out here," he said. Not quite an apology. It was his office after all.

"Yes, I was. I mean, I am. I'm new," she fumbled for the right words.

Cooper let his gaze drop from Ro's face and travel quickly down her whole body, taking in her dress, her shoes, her shape. His eyes were dark with heavy lids. She couldn't tell if he was tired or if this sexy, sleepy look was his permanent expression. He had a thick 5 o'clock shadow and his hair was uncombed. When he lifted his eyes to hers again she felt a tickle deep in her belly.

"Are you my new secretary?" He asked. The deep tones of his voice sent another, sharper, tickle through the center of her body.

She nodded. Then reconsidered and asked, "Are you Mr. Rivera?"

He smiled, revealing perfect teeth, perfect dimples, and a

perfect smile. He reached towards her to shake her hand, "Cooper."

"I'm Rowan Murray," she took his hand and shook it, trying to ignore how his strong, warm grip pleased her. "People usually call me 'Ro'."

"Ro," he repeated, seeming to roll the idea of her name over in his mind. Then he dropped her hand and said, "Okay, Ro. I'm going for a swim."

"All right, I'll be here."

He grinned at her, "I hope so. Oh, and people usually call me 'Coop'." Then he turned away, giving her a little wink as he did, and sauntered out the front door.

Ro watched him go. The initial shock of their meeting was over, yet it took a while for her nerves to settle.

Cooper didn't return, not that afternoon anyway.

Ro kept herself busy. Waiting for him to return from his swim with a towel hung jauntily around his neck, drops of water still clinging to his sculpted chest. But she waited in vain. When 5 o'clock rolled around she reluctantly shut down her laptop and left the office. A small but noticeable piece of her was quite disappointed.

Her first work day officially over, she joined Gloria for a light dinner in the dining room. Then, finally, Ro was alone in her room with her thoughts. And what thoughts they were.

She flopped down on her bed face up, her arms stretched out to either side. She was elated, ecstatic, exhausted. It had only been 24 hours ago that she'd landed at the airport and jostled to find a taxi to take her to Playa del Carmen. Just this morning she'd been nervously getting ready to interview, not sure she would be offered a job at all.

But now.

Now she was in her very own elegant room, working in a luxury hotel, the secretary for one of the most attractive, wealthy, mysterious men she'd ever met in person. Winston used to always tell her, "My cup runneth over." And now she knew what he meant.

Winston. She wanted to call him and tell him everything that had happened. She should probably call her mother, too, just to check in. First she'd need to fish her phone out of her purse and find her charger.

Her phone.

Ro paused.

She hadn't looked at her phone, or checked her Instagram for pictures of Theo and his fiancé, all day long.

She smiled at this realization. A happy buzzing sensation filled her head and heart. And then, before she could make herself get up and retrieve her purse from the chair in the corner of the room, Ro fell asleep.

Chapter Four

Knock, knock, knock.

The sound drifted into her mind, not quite registering.

Knock, knock, knock.

Again.

Ro turned her head on her pillow. The deep gentle feeling of being comfortably asleep came into her consciousness. Then it was gone.

Knock, knock, knock.

"Hello?" A man's voice from the other side of the door.

Her eyes opened. She glanced around the dimly lit room, not sure at first where she was. Then, as the fog of sleep lifted and she remembered that she was in her new room at the Hotel Diamante, the light knock and the man's voice came again.

Knock, knock, knock.

"Señorita? It's Carlos."

Her first thought was that there was an emergency. From what she could see out her windows it was not yet morning.

She couldn't think of another reason why Carlos would be knocking at her door in the middle of the night.

Ro reluctantly sat up on the edge of the bed. A murmur of voices outside her door made her even more curious. One of the voices sounded like a child.

She padded across the floor to the door and looked through the peephole. She could see Carlos standing with a woman. The tops of two children's heads were just visible. The woman was speaking to Carlos, but Ro couldn't hear what was being said. Maybe she should just ignore them and go back to bed. She wasn't due to work until 9:00 am, and it had to be before 6:00 am. The sun hadn't come up yet.

A nugget of fear sat in her stomach. She'd just met Carlos. She wasn't sure she knew him well enough to open her door to him at this hour.

Knock, knock, knock.

There it was again. Not too loud. It must not be an emergency.

"It's Carlos. We go to beach..."

The beach? This peaked her curiosity. The nugget of fear dissolved and she unlocked the door, pulling it back cautiously.

"Buenos dias, Señorita," Carlos said, beaming at her. He had one hand on the woman's back and one hand on a little boy's head, maybe seven or eight years old, who stood in front of him. A little girl, younger than the boy by a few years, held tightly to the woman's hand. "Sorry to awake you," His brow furrowed at the sight of her rumpled look.

"It's fine, is everything okay?" Ro answered, trying to sound like she hadn't just woken up.

"It's good, thank you. This is my family," his smile grew even larger, if that was possible.

Ro raised her eyebrows, surprised and pleased, "Oh, hello."

The woman nodded her head in greeting, smiled shyly, but didn't speak. The little boy smiled widely at her. He looked very much like his father, Ro noticed. The girl pressed herself into her mother's skirt, watching Ro with big eyes.

"My wife, Josefina. My son, Jorge. My daughter, Francisca," Carlos continued with the introductions despite the rather unusual circumstances.

"Nice to meet you," Ro said, smiling at all three of them.

"We go to beach each morning to walk," Carlos continued. "You come with us? Or," he looked for the right English phrase, "You like to come with us?"

"Oh!" He was inviting her to the beach with his family. How wonderful! Ro's polite smile became a full-blown look of delight, "Yes, I would like to come with you."

Carlos looked even more delighted than she felt. He said something quickly in Spanish to Josefina and the woman smiled and nodded warmly.

"You meet us in front of hotel?"

"Yes, yes," Ro glanced down at her wrinkled sundress. She'd been so tired last night she hadn't even changed into pajamas. "I'll change clothes and meet you there in...10 minutes?"

"10 minutes," Carlos annunciated the words carefully, nodding emphatically.

20 minutes later Ro was strolling onto the white sand beach of Playa del Carmen escorted by her very own tour guides.

Though warm enough to wear shorts, the absence of the sun left the temperature a comfortable cool. Ro had quickly pulled on a pair of khaki shorts, a Bob Ross T-shirt that was one of her favorites, and her red Indiana University pullover sweatshirt. With her hair up in a fast pony tail and no makeup, she felt like a little kid on an adventure.

Though the sun was not up quite yet, its presence was

obvious. Since Carlos had first knocked on her door until now, the sky had turned from deep purple to a lighter purple with a reddish glow growing on the ocean horizon. Ro had been to the oceans in California and along the East coast and Florida several times. She always loved the feeling of walking into a wide-open space with nothing but blue water stretching out for as far as the eye could see.

In this case, on the Caribbean ocean, the water was especially blue. Even with the limited light of the coming sunrise, the turquoise color shimmered across the surface. The white sand that stretched along the water's edge was muted in the pale light and broken in places by black silhouettes of scattered palm trees or the occasional pile of kelp or beach chair. A few other people were out, taking in the pre-dawn sky, but not too many. Ro thought the beach probably filled up considerably after the sun came up.

"Carlos!" A man's voice came to them from somewhere near the water.

Carlos turned and peered at the silhouetted form that jogged towards them. Then, recognition, and Carlos waved enthusiastically, "Señor Zander!"

At the mention of the newcomer's name, both children left their parent's sides and ran towards the figure, shouting happily. As the figure got closer Ro could see it was a man, medium height, wearing a pair of pink and green board shorts. He had long, bleached out hair that he wore in flopping dread locks and a curly, bleached blonde beard. He laughed and talked to the children and Ro could hear his Australian accent even though she couldn't quite make out the words.

"How're you doin', mate?" The man said warmly when he reached them, sticking out his hand to shake Carlos'.

"Good, good, Señor," Carlos said. He introduced Ro and

Zander, explaining that she was now working for Mr. Rivera, and they shook hands. Zander's hand was rough with a strong grip, but his eyes were what she noticed most. Pale blue, almost like crystals. They were what she would call piercing blue eyes even in the not-quite daylight.

"Ah, an expat are you?" Zander asked, his brilliant eyes smiling at her.

"Yes, brand new," she answered.

"You'll love it here. It's absolute paradise," he said as he gave the shoreline and rising sun a sweeping gaze.

Sunrise was growing nearer. The horizon was glowing and turning the sky above them from purple to dark pink. More light shone across the water, pulling out its bright blue and showing off the white bubbly edge of the waves as they rolled up onto the sand then retreated, leaving a shining, flat surface behind.

"It really is, isn't it?" Ro said, more to herself than anyone. She looked back at Zander who was grinning at her, and asked, "What do you do here?"

"I run a little dive shop, give scuba tours."

"That must be fun."

"It is. Do you scuba?" He asked. She shook her head 'no'. Zander's smile deepened and he nudged her arm with his elbow, "You should try it."

The thought of diving into the turquoise water and sinking far underneath, exploring the coral reefs, seeing the tropical fish and plants, swimming free under the water like she belonged there, filled her with both excitement and trepidation. She should learn how to scuba dive. She cocked her head sideways and gave Zander a bright smile.

"I might take you up on that!"

They all stood together taking in the gorgeous colors that filled the sky, the rhythmic sound of the waves swishing against the sand, and the scent of fresh salty air. Zander and Carlos chatted about a few things as Josefina kept a keen eye on her children who were racing back and forth between the adults and the waves. Without any Spanish skills there was little Ro could talk about with Josefina, but she still felt a warm camaraderie between them as the women in the group. Content to appreciate the sunrise and the laughing children together.

Ro glanced at Josefina's profile. She was a pretty woman. Dark skin, beautiful thick, black hair, and large dark eyes. Ro reminded herself that she needed to get that online Spanish tutorial software today. She didn't want to miss out on getting to know people because of her lack of language skills.

In the distance, a movement caught her eye and Ro shifted her attention to the form of a man walking towards them along the beach. Something about his movement was familiar. He was tall and lean, with wide shoulders. He was wearing a white, untucked button down shirt and what looked like knee length cargo shorts. In the muted light she couldn't exactly see his face, mostly just his form walking intently towards them.

Cooper? Her stomach did a flip-flop at the thought, and her heart rate increased slightly. In that split second Ro knew she might have a problem if she felt that kind of nervous attraction to her brand new boss. She told herself to relax and just go with the flow. He was simply a super rich, jet setting, gorgeous man who she was most likely going to get to know extremely well being his personal administrative assistant. No worries, as her new acquaintance, Zander, might say.

The man came closer and Ro could make out his face.

Not Cooper.

Her mouth dropped open. She couldn't believe what she was seeing. She gave her head a little shake, blinking her eyes. Maybe the man was a mirage or something.

But, no.

He saw her now, too, and lifted his arm in an enthusiastic wave, calling her name, "Ro!"

Her eyes were wide with surprise. And though Ro's mouth was still open, she was too astounded to return his greeting.

Chapter Five

"I found you!" Winston declared, both joy and relief on his face.

"Winston? What are you doing here?" Ro stepped away from her small group to meet him. Astonished at the sight of him.

"I'm on vacation!" He opened his arms as if embracing the entire ocean sunrise moment. He laughed at her surprised expression, put his hands on her shoulders and then pulled her into a hug.

She hugged him back. Still in shock, but happy to see him. She was always happy to see Winston.

He squeezed her closer than any of the friendly hugs they'd shared at work. Longer too.

"I don't understand," she said into his shoulder.

He pulled away and held her at arms length, "I took a month off!"

Ro was nothing short of baffled.

"But...you don't go on vacations," was all she could think to say.

He let go of her shoulders and looked down at the sand sheepishly, then lifted his gaze to hers. The first rays of the sun spread brilliant orange and pink light across his face, making his usually plain brown eyes shine. He hadn't shaved and the stubble, combined with his messy hair and wrinkled shirt, gave him a casual look. Like they'd been on a road trip together, or stayed out all night after a concert. Although, they had never done anything of the sort.

"And you normally answer your phone," he said. It wasn't a reprimand, just an explanation. She gasped and covered her mouth with her hand. She'd forgotten about calling him last night. She'd forgotten about calling anyone.

"Oh my God! I'm so sorry!"

Of course, he would have been worried about her. Everyone was probably worried about her. Her parents!

Winston half shrugged and looked out at the bright orange orb that was lifting slowly over the ocean, lighting up the water and beach and everything around them with a golden glow.

"It's not bad as rescue missions go," he said.

Ro turned away, distraught, "I need to call my Mom!"

"Here," Winston had his cell in his hand, it was dialing. The contact name read 'Margaret Ro's Mom'.

She grabbed the phone from him just in time to hear her Mom's worried voice.

For ten minutes Ro talked her Mom down. She had been worried sick and filled Ro in on how she had contacted Winston through Facebook because she knew they were close and thought maybe he had heard from Ro in Mexico. Once Winston knew that her parents hadn't heard from her either, he tried to get in touch with her, but she never answered the calls or texts. Her Dad had been packing a bag to fly to Playa del Carmen and find her when Winston stepped in. He told her parents that he had tons of vacation time and would go himself, saving them the extra expense. Ro knew that Winston was aware her parents weren't very well off. It was one of the many things she'd shared with him over the years.

"He insisted on going," her mother told her.

"He did?" She glanced at Winston who had joined her small group as she'd stepped away to speak on the phone. He was shaking hands with Carlos.

"Yes, thank goodness he found you. What a nice young man," her mother continued.

Ro paced up and down the white sand, talking to her Mom for a few more minutes and then her Dad. Meanwhile, Winston chatted with Carlos and Zander. She saw that he even managed a few short sentences of Spanish with Josefina and the two children. Ro didn't know that Winston could speak Spanish.

Satisfied that their daughter hadn't been kidnapped by a drug cartel or sold into human slavery, her Mom eventually let her hang up. Ro promised she would call her this evening after work.

Work. It was getting late in the morning. She needed to get ready for her first real day on the job. As she returned to the group, Ro heard the tail end of a conversation.

"Of course you will stay at Hotel Diamante," Carlos was saying.

"I would love to," Winston said, glancing at her as he did.

She smiled and thanked him for the use of his phone, handing it back to him. When he took it from her, his hand wrapped around hers for a moment. She found all of this touching strange. She and Winston had been work friends for years and they had never touched this much. His presence here was disconcerting, too. Like a puzzle piece that just didn't fit because it belonged to a totally different puzzle, he didn't belong here in her new life. There was no space for him.

"Everything good?" Winston asked, "You look ticked off."

He was right. She was scowling.

"No, I'm fine," she said. But she wasn't. And Winston knew she wasn't. He knew her very well.

HER FIRST FULL day at her new job started much like the day before had ended. Ro sat alone in her small, beautiful office, quietly musing at what was going on behind the closed double doors. Waiting to be discovered again by her new boss. Certain she would handle it more gracefully than she had yesterday.

She tried to ignore the fact that her hair was still damp from taking a shower a little later than planned. And the fact that she still didn't have dressing for work in this hot and humid climate quite down. Ro had been forced to put aside all of the work clothes she'd brought with her because the material just wasn't suitable. Either light and silky rayon or heavier polyester blends were simply not wearable here.

Luckily, she'd brought enough cotton clothes to get her through the week. Today she wore a bohemian style ankle length skirt in a burnt orange floral print and a plain white short sleeve button up shirt. It was passible, but a little too far on the casual side for her liking. She would need to do some shopping if she was planning on staying here for good.

And stay was exactly what Ro was going to do.

If she hadn't been sure about it yesterday when Alicia showed her into this elegant, beautiful room that would be her office, she had been sure the moment she stepped onto the beach this morning. The fresh, salty smell, the cool breeze in her face, the way the sky changed into brilliant colors right in front of her eyes, the feeling of abandon, like she'd stepped into her real life after waking from a long sleep. The last time she'd felt anything like it had been when she met Theo.

"And this is all me, nothing to do with him," she said under her breath.

She stood up and went to the window to pull up the thick wooden blinds. She loved the way the light filtered through the heavy glass as well as the view. The bustling life in the street below made the scene vibrant.

The double doors clicked behind her and Ro whirled around just as Cooper stuck his head out of his office. Seeing her, he smiled, but didn't move any further into the room.

"You're here," he said happily.

"I'm here," she answered.

"Can you help me with something?"

Ro nodded and moved towards him, "Of course." Her words were choked a little with nerves, but she managed to gather herself together while she crossed the room.

When she got to the double doors, he pulled them open to reveal an exquisite office worthy of any Fortune 500 CEO or five-star hotel owner. The room was at least double the size of her office and the waiting area combined. The rich dark wood accents, prevalent throughout the hotel in every beam, in all of the trim, and in the intricately carved crown molding, was still center stage in this room. But here in Cooper's office the wood craftsmanship had been taken to another level.

The ceiling was at least ten feet high and every inch of it was covered with the deep brown shining wood. Beams of it had been carefully carved and fit together into square frames inside larger square frames three times over, creating a deep relief effect that was gorgeous. Ro had never seen a coffered ceiling quite like this, in fact she'd rarely seen one in person anywhere until now.

There were bookshelves, a large executive desk and small, ornate tables placed tastefully throughout the room. There was an imposing leather rolling chair behind the desk and comfortable looking wine colored chairs in a generous sitting area. A few large paintings with tiny canned lights trained on them from above and below graced the walls. Ro didn't know much about art, but she guessed these were expensive pieces.

Despite the fact that the room dripped with money and power, Ro struggled to take it all in or be impressed by it in any way. Her struggle stemmed from the fact that Cooper stood in front of her wearing perfectly tailored black slacks and absolutely nothing else. No shoes or socks and, most distracting of all, no shirt.

"What do you think?" He asked, holding up two hangers that held white tuxedo shirts with slightly different designs so she could see them.

"Um," Ro blinked hard, trying to tear her eyes away from Cooper's naked chest, muscled biceps and the tops of his shoulders that were flexing as he held up the shirts. "What jacket are you going to wear?" It was all she could think of to buy more time.

Cooper grinned at her, "Smart girl." He gave her the shirts to hold and stepped to a rolling clothing rack that held several different tuxedo jackets, multiple vests in different colors and what looked like a variety of cummerbunds and bow ties. He grabbed two black jackets and lifted them up as he had the shirts. Displaying them for her to see.

"For the party," Cooper said. Of course, the New Year's Eve party.

Ro liked how he spoke to her as if they'd known each other forever, as if there was no question that she knew exactly what he was talking about. She looked carefully at the two jackets. One was a classic cut with shining black satin lapels. The other was double breasted and looked like it would barely fit over his muscular chest. Both would look fantastic on him. Anything would look fantastic on him. Images from the internet of Cooper wearing his untucked, unbuttoned tuxedo shirt flashed through her mind and she lost focus again.

"This one is new," Cooper indicated the double-breasted jacket in his right hand with a quick nod.

"Hmmm," Ro nodded, pretending this new bit of information made a difference. She couldn't make a choice. Either one would be amazing. Anyway, she was having a hard time processing the fact that she was in this room giving her opinion to this beautiful man to begin with.

"Hello?" A voice carried to them from outside the double doors.

Someone was in the waiting room. She and Cooper looked toward the door then back to each other. Even though there was nothing vaguely intimate going on, Ro couldn't help but feel that they were somehow about to be caught in a risqué situation. She opened her mouth to excuse herself and take care of her reception duties when Winston poked his head into the open double doors.

"Hello," he said again, grinning.

Ro's embarrassment was just slightly outweighed by irritation. She glared at him.

Cooper looked lazily back and forth between she and Winston, his gaze finally landing on her, "Is this a friend of yours?"

Ro nodded, feeling ridiculously unprofessional, "This is Winston, he's a friend from my old job." To her surprise, Cooper smiled widely at Winston and motioned him into the room. Winston came in without hesitation and joined her. Ro refused to look at him.

"All right, my brother, what do you think?" Cooper held the two jackets up even higher so both she and Winston could see them well.

Winston considered the two jackets while Ro fumed. Why did he have to butt his head into the first real interaction she was having with her new hot, shirtless boss? Her fuming turned to mortification when Winston gave a 'meh' face and shrugged, effectively dismissing both jacket choices.

"Really?" Cooper seemed surprised and turned the jackets towards himself to look for whatever offense Winston saw in them.

"They're not bad," Winston said casually. Ro's eyebrows raised in disbelief. "But that one is gonna be too warm," Winston pointed at the double-breasted jacket. "If you're planning on wearing it around here," he added.

Cooper nodded in understanding, "True."

Winston's eyes wandered across the other options that hung on the rolling rack. Ro tried to think of something intelligent or classy or funny to say, but she was drawing a blank. All she could think about was the fact that Winston, wearing a pair of board shorts with a pink and green palm tree print, a bright yellow Corona beer T-shirt that he'd obviously just bought in the gift shop, and a pair of purple flip flops, was giving fashion advice to the man who might be the most perfect man she'd ever met.

She needed to get Winston out of here. Push him out the door so she could retrieve the moment with Cooper. She was about to say something, anything, when Winston abruptly went to the clothing rack and pulled out a gold tuxedo jacket with black lapels and cuffs.

"What about this one?"

Her initial reaction was to laugh. Who would wear a gold tuxedo? She stifled this reaction when she saw Cooper's expression. He was smiling broadly, obviously taken with Winston's idea.

"Yeah?" Cooper went to the rack and abandoned the two black jackets, taking the gold one to inspect.

Ro's vision of sipping a glass of champagne with Cooper dressed in his classy black tuxedo jacket fizzled. She could see that the gold jacket idea had peaked his interest. He took it off the hanger and put it on. With his bare chest and black slacks he looked a lot like an exotic male dancer, which wasn't necessarily a bad thing.

"What do you think?" Cooper turned towards her and posed with his arms reaching out a little, as if he was about to walk up to her and give her a hug.

She swallowed. It wasn't that he looked bad in the gold jacket. He looked amazing. But her first choice would have been the black one. Nerves filled her stomach. She felt heat rise in her cheeks and was embarrassed at being embarrassed. Why was she struggling so hard with this situation? Ro flicked her eyes to Winston who stood cool and confident behind Cooper. His presence was making her feel uncertain. It reminded her of her old life. The one she wanted to forget.

Both of the men were waiting for her response. She was overthinking. She had to say something.

"Sure," she said, nodding.

Then Ro did something that surprised her. It surprised Winston, too, she could tell by the look on his face. She moved to Cooper so that she was standing directly in front of him, looking up into his chiseled, handsome face. She put her hands on his shoulders, smoothing the material, which was softer than she had thought it would be, then let her hands run down the length of both of his arms, as if she was evaluating the cut. Cooper grinned down at her, amused. And, she could tell, a little turned on.

She smiled back at him and said, "It's nice."

"Thanks," Cooper said, his voice was deep and sensual. It reverberated through her. He smelled good, too.

Then, because apparently he was bent on interrupting her world, Winston chimed in, "Good choice. Now that that's decided, Ro, wanna have lunch with me?"

It took everything she had not to roll her eyes.

Chapter Six

"It's just that the hotel is throwing a huge New Year's Eve party tomorrow night and I won't have a lot of time," Ro explained.

She and Winston were seated at one of the corner tables in the hotel dining room. An employee and a guest eating lunch together. Ro wasn't sure if this was the kind of thing that would be deeply frowned upon by Alicia. She was pretty sure Cooper was fine with it, since he'd insisted that she make plans with Winston while they were all choosing his tuxedo in his office earlier. Her new boss had even gone so far as to send them a complimentary bottle of wine during their meal.

"Enjoy lunch, Coop," Winston had read the note that came with the bottle out loud. Then he raised one eyebrow, "Coop?"

"That's what people call him," Ro said defensively.

She'd felt defensive the entire lunch. When Winston pulled her chair out for her as they were being seated, when he asked her how her first full day was going, when he'd ordered the chicken with chili and dark chocolate sauce for them both...in Spanish. Everything he did prickled at her nerves, which was why she was trying to explain to him that she was going to be too busy to hang out with him before he went home. She was going to be working a lot on the party.

"What about after the party?" He asked, taking another bite of the creamy caramel covered flan on his plate.

"Well, I think I'm going to be pretty wiped out after the party."

Winston chuckled, "No, not right after the party. What about a day or two after the party? Will you have any time off then?"

Ro looked at him blankly.

"But you won't be here," she said.

"Of course I'll be here," Winston said, lifting his wine glass and looking appreciatively around the dining patio. "I'm on vacation!" He toasted the air and took a sip of his wine.

"But you don't take vacations," Ro continued to be stunned into making stupid comments.

"I do now," Winston said, scooping up another large spoonful of flan. "I'm not gonna fly right back after I just got here. I'm gonna look around a little, have some fun," he put the giant bite into his mouth and wiggled his eyebrows at her.

The general irritation she'd been feeling towards him escalated into full-blown anxiety. How long was he planning on staying here? Would he be constantly interrupting her new life? Did he expect her to tag along with him on this vacation fun?

"How long?" She asked the question quietly, looking down and pushing her flan around with the back side of her spoon. Her enthusiasm for dessert was dissipating.

"I took a month off from work," he said.

"You're staying a month?" She looked up at him in shock, then dropped her eyes again. Trying to hide her disappointment.

"You're upset," Winston said, dipping his head and trying to look up into her lowered gaze.

"I'm not upset."

"You are," he gave her a charming smile. Ro put down her spoon and looked away. "Don't worry, I'm not gonna hang around you like a loser," he nudged her foot under the table with the toe of his sandal.

Relieved, and a little ashamed at how relieved she was, Ro looked back at him. Winston had dressed up a little for lunch. He wore new leather all sport sandals, a white short sleeved light cotton shirt with wood buttons and a pair of olive green cargo shorts. He had been swimming and shopping for clothes while he waited for lunch to roll around, and a twinge of tropical color had taken the edge off of his normal Midwestern pallor.

"I don't mean to ignore you, Winston, I just...I just..." she couldn't explain. She didn't want to hurt his feelings. He'd come all this way to check on her, and he was her friend.

"You just want to start your new life, I got it," Winston picked up the wine bottle. There was only a little bit left and he offered it to Ro. She shook her head 'no'. This was the middle of her work day after all. Winston poured the last of the wine into his glass as he spoke, "I was talking to that Zander guy, from Australia. I think I'm gonna to take some scuba lessons. Check out the local sights. Maybe go to see some ruins!"

The image of Winston, accountant extraordinaire, making his way through the tropical beauty of the area with a map and a pair of binoculars popped into Ro's mind. She giggled.

"What? I think the ruins would be intriguing," he said.

This made her laugh again.

"Go ahead, laugh all you want. I don't get to live here forever like you do. I gotta get in some rest and relaxation type fun before I head back to the rat race."

"You should," she said, and she meant it.

"I'll find something we can do together," he started, then held up his palm to stop her from speaking, "In a few days, I know, I know. It'll take me that long to find something fun enough to pull you away from Tuxedo Man."

She laughed again, a genuine laugh.

Gloria appeared at her side just as she got over her giggle fit.

"Señorita Ro," Gloria said, giving Winston a smile and nod as she did.

"Yes?" Ro sat up straighter. Gloria may be a grey haired lady in a flowing rose print dress, but she was basically Alicia's right hand. She got, and deserved, all of Ro's most respectful attention.

"We will meet in your office at one o'clock?" Gloria asked.

"Yes, absolutely. You were going to give me all of my tasks for tomorrow's party," Ro said.

Gloria nodded, "That's good." Her fine eyebrows knit together as she let her gaze run up and down Ro's outfit. For a moment, Ro thought the older woman was going to call her out for her casual attire. Instead, Gloria asked, "Do you have a dress for the party? It is a formal event."

Ro's heart sank. She hadn't thought about what she would wear to the party. Even if more of her wardrobe was suitable to this climate, she hadn't brought anything remotely formal. Gloria read the expression on her face and placed her hand on Ro's shoulder.

"I will take you shopping tonight after work? I know the best dress shops," Gloria told her.

"Yes, thank you. That's very nice of you," Ro gushed.

"A pretty young woman should have a pretty new dress for such a big party," Gloria said. Her eyes smiled kindly at Ro, then she gave Winston a meaningful look. He lifted his eyebrows, understanding that the nice old lady must think he was Ro's date or maybe even her boyfriend. That was not the kind of rumor Ro wanted to get spread around the hotel. She started to correct her, but Gloria had already turned and was walking smoothly towards the dining area exit.

"Maybe you could get something in gold," Winston said, giving her an exaggerated wink.

This time she did roll her eyes at him.

By the time she and Gloria could finally step away from party preparations and go dress shopping, Ro was afraid it was too late and the best places would be closed. Though the sun hadn't gone down, it was definitely on its way. She sat in the back seat of a small taxi cab, watching the streets full of tourists and locals, bicycles, carts and more cabs, as they buzzed past. Gloria sat next to her, looking even smaller than normal because her chin barely reached the bottom of the cab window. The size of a child, she gazed out her open window, letting the breeze flow against her face.

Ro was exhausted. Their whole afternoon had been a whirlwind. There were so many details to take care of, and without knowing the language, most of Ro's duties had been of the run and fetch, or spit and polish variety. She had helped count and set up all of the silver centerpieces and candelabras so they were ready to dress the room before breakfast opened tomorrow morning, making sure they were all polished and up to snuff as she did. She had also helped decide where the floral arrangements would go and drew out a map for Carlos to have ready for the florist when they arrived.

With food deliveries tripling today and tomorrow, Carlos was overwhelmed, so Ro had also helped out at the front desk. She was the official greeter of anyone speaking English, which was fun. She didn't mind the happy chatter of tourists. In fact, it made her feel good when they were impressed that she worked there, and lived there, full time. Of course, she didn't tell any of them that she'd only been in Playa del Carmen a few days.

At first, she'd been concerned that maybe Cooper would be looking for her in her office. So she asked Gloria.

"It's okay with Coop- I mean, Mr. Rivera, that I'm away from my desk, isn't it?"

"Mr. Rivera takes little interest in business matters when a party is on the schedule," Alicia answered coldly. She was standing nearby and had overheard the question. She gave Ro a withering look. Ro didn't know if Alicia's disdain was because of Cooper's lack of interest in hotel business, or if it was the fact that she'd called him by his first name. Or both.

When everything had wrapped up for the day, Gloria had taken her by the arm and directed her out the front door past the crystal fountain in front of the hotel to a waiting cab. The cabbie, a small, wrinkled Mexican man with a huge grey mustache, straightened up when he saw Gloria approaching. Funny that she had that effect on everyone.

"Señora, Señorita," the cabbie gave them each a small bow before opening the door for them to slip in. Ro got the feeling that Gloria knew the cabbie, or at least he knew who Gloria was and held her in some esteem. When they arrived at the boutique dress shop called 'Luna Rica', that feeling was reinforced.

Not only were they greeted with a flurry of attention from three beautifully dressed mature women who spilled out the front door when their cab pulled up, but the cabbie didn't drive away in search of more patrons. Instead, he opened their doors, offered his hand to help them out of the cab, then discreetly parked up against the side of the small building and waited for them. More like a chauffeur than a cabbie.

The boutique ladies bustled Ro and Gloria inside. The air was nicely temperature controlled, several gorgeous beaded evening gowns were displayed on mannequins, which were lined up along the side walls under spotlights, making them sparkle. The back wall was covered with floor to ceiling mirrors set at angles against one another so anyone standing in front of them could get a view of every inch of their body.

The three ladies sat them down in two wingback chairs that faced the mirrors and Ro was thankful for the comfortable elegance of this place. The ladies all spoke Spanish with Gloria, murmuring quietly and taking turns leaving then returning with refreshments. They brought a white, milky, sweet drink that was cold, smooth and delicious. Gloria told Ro it was called horchata. They also brought them tiny, bite-sized empanadas that were like small corn calzones full of different savory meats.

Munching her empanadas and sipping her horchata, Ro thought she had died and gone to heaven. And after a few minutes of being cooed over and fed, she was rejuvenated enough to notice more of her surroundings.

For a dress shop there were very few dresses on display. Although, those that she could see from her chair were absolutely stunning. Not really dresses, but rather gowns. Statements.

The three boutique ladies were almost exactly the same size, no variation in height or age from what Ro could tell. They were soft and feminine, curvy without being overweight. Graceful. Though their dresses were feminine and flowing, like Gloria's, they all wore black or grey or a mix thereof instead of the pretty pastels that Ro had seen in Gloria's floral prints.

Gloria noticed Ro peering around the edge of her winged

chair trying to look at the dresses, the women and their surroundings. Gloria smiled sweetly and nodded at one of the boutique ladies. Suddenly there was a flurry of activity and all three ladies disappeared behind the mirrors.

Ro wondered if she should get up and look around, perhaps take a dress into a dressing room and try it on. Before she had a chance to move, a teenage girl emerged from behind the mirrors. She was slender, not too tall, about Ro's height and size, and she was wearing a gorgeous deep green evening gown. With a princess neckline and a drop waist, the gown moved sensually as the young woman walked. Ro saw the girl looking at her and quickly looked away, not realizing, yet, that the girl was modeling the dress for her.

"You don't like this one?" Gloria asked.

"Oh," Ro shook her head and blushed a little, "I didn't know she was showing me."

"Yes, this is for you. It's less tiring this way," Gloria explained. She leaned back in her wing-backed chair and took a sip of her horchata. So, Ro followed suit, and turned a more critical eye on the green dress.

She liked the flow of it, but the color wasn't really her favorite and it wasn't as sparkly as some of the others along the wall. The girl walked back and forth in front of them, pausing and turning slowly each time she turned around. This was the first time Ro had shopped in this manner, like someone who came from wealth. She wasn't sure what the protocol was for refusing a dress. She tried to think of a way to say it without being insulting to the dress or the model.

"It's very lovely, but I'm not sure this one is for me," she said.

Gloria nodded and swished her hand in a curt dismissive manner to the model. The girl turned on her heel and went quickly away. A surprisingly short time later, no more than 30 seconds, the girl returned wearing a form fitted black cocktail dress. This dress definitely had sparkles, sequins were sewn all over the bodice and in a swirling pattern that dipped down from the waist onto the hipline. But the spaghetti straps and very low cut neckline made Ro a little nervous. She didn't want to come across too sexy at her first official office party.

This time Gloria read her expression and Ro barely had to move her head before Gloria was sending the girl away. Quick as a wink she was back, this time in a gold gown. Ro smiled to herself. She couldn't go gold. It would be too weird.

After four more attempts Ro was beginning to think she might need to be less picky. Maybe she should have tried on the light blue dress or the very first one they showed her, the green one. Maybe it was all too much after her long day and the incredibly eventful last few days of flying here and getting the job and everything. Perhaps she was hopeless and would have to wear her cotton sundress to the party.

Then she saw the red dress.

Ro was immediately drawn to the color. A poppy red, bright and fresh, yet still sexy. Sleeveless, with a scoop neck, the cut was relatively simple. Fitted to the body without clinging or being too tight, the dress was fuller starting at the knees, which gave it a flirty kick when the girl was walking.

The feature that really got Ro's attention, however, was the beadwork. Sewn in overlapping patterns using diamond shapes of different sizes, the dress almost looked like something from the 1920's, the way it shimmered in the light. Ro sat up straighter as the girl turned in front of her, giving her the best view of the back, which was much lower than the front and showed off the girl's shoulder blades and smooth skin.

"I think perhaps this is your dress," Gloria said. She nodded at the girl and within minutes Ro was in the dressing room looking at her reflection. The dress was on and fit almost perfectly. Any alterations were being efficiently calculated, discussed and pinned by the three boutique ladies. Gloria watched from a comfortable chair in the corner of the dressing room, smiling widely.

"This is perfect for you. It's elegant, beautiful and fun," Gloria said.

Ro agreed. Looking in the mirror she was filled with the kind of excitement she used to feel when her parents were taking her to the amusement park in the summer, or when they left on a trip early in the morning. Her stomach filled with that same fluttering thrill and she marveled at how she'd ended up here, in this dress, preparing for the biggest party she'd ever been to in her life. She'd never had a dress like this. She'd never been able to afford it.

The fluttering in her stomach suddenly twisted into a knot and made her feel sick. She hadn't thought about how much this dress would cost. This kind of boutique was so high end. Even if they gave her a good deal because Gloria was obviously a good customer, she doubted she could afford this beautiful dress.

Gloria and the head boutique lady spoke rapidly in Spanish. Sealing the deal no doubt.

"They will make the alterations and deliver it to the hotel tomorrow before noon," Gloria informed her.

"I'm sorry, I didn't think to ask about the price," Ro said. "I'm not sure I can afford such a beautiful dress."

Gloria waved away Ro's comment, "We will charge it to the hotel. Your hiring bonus, yes?"

Too stunned to answer immediately, Ro finally swallowed hard and answered, "Yes."

Yes. Absolutely.

Before she knew it, her mind conjured up an image of Cooper in his gold tuxedo jacket, and she smiled. Red and gold went well together.

Chapter Seven

Winston looked excited and nervous, like a little boy about to embark on a new adventure. He was paying strict attention to Zander's instructions, his eyes bright with the new challenge of scuba diving.

Ro, on the other hand, wasn't really listening. Zander was going over the rules of diving, the things to look out for, the possible dangers, how to safely ascend, decompression sickness, but it was going in one ear and out the other. She had only come with Winston to see him off, intent on getting to her office on time today and, hopefully, spending some time with Cooper before the big party. Of course it would be work time, not like a date or anything, but still.

"What do you think?" Winston asked. He posed in the wetsuit he'd pulled on over his board shorts.

Ro eyed him up and down. The slick black look flattered him, actually. The way the material clung to his body accentuated his build and she was surprised to see that Winston had fairly wide shoulders. She had never noticed that when he was in his everyday clothes. He looked bigger in a wetsuit.

"He looks like a shark!" Zander exclaimed. He was

carrying scuba gear to a low empty table, getting it ready to haul to the boat.

Zander's dive shop was actually a garage, with a cement floor and metal walls and roof. But it was clean, with all kinds of scuba and snorkeling gear hanging on iron bars that looked like they'd been built specifically for this space and then attached to the metal walls. The front door, which was a garage door, was fully open to the beach and the dock where his boat waited, allowing the full sunrise of Playa del Carmen to shine into the building.

Ro had been taking a morning stroll on the beach with Carlos and his family when they ran into Winston on his way to Zander's place. It was just a short walk down the beach to the dive shop, so Ro had joined him to offer her support.

"You sure you don't want to come?" Zander asked her, his piercing blue eyes glittering with fun.

"No, I can't. I have to work," she answered. She tried to look disappointed, not wanting to insult Zander. In truth she was thrilled to go to work today. Not only would she probably, maybe, hopefully, see Cooper, she had the added pleasure of knowing that the day would end with her wearing her gorgeous new dress to the New Year's Eve party.

"On a day like this? It's the last day of the year and it's gonna be a beauty," Zander said. He swept his arm towards the sand and water and sunrise outside the open garage door as proof. "All work and no play..." Zander grinned at her.

"Well, in all fairness, I've only worked at the hotel a few days, I don't think I could ask for any time off just yet," Ro explained. The ocean was enticing there was no doubt about it, but she wasn't just a tourist here. She had responsibilities...and plans.

"Right, you're working for Coop aren't you?" Zander asked.

Winston gave Ro a look, raising his eyebrows at the

mention of Cooper's nickname. She scowled at his silent teasing.

"Yes, and we've got the big party tonight and everything," she answered.

"Ah, yeah, he puts on a great party," Zander mused. He chuckled to himself, remembering parties past no doubt.

"Are you going?" Winston asked Zander.

Zander shrugged.

"Are you?" Zander asked Winston, "You're staying there, aren't you?"

"I might," Winston looked at Ro, checking her reaction.

"You don't need my permission," Ro said. She never said he couldn't do whatever he wanted to do while he was here.

Now it was Winston's turn to shrug.

"I just want to be sure not to interrupt you at work," Winston said. He looked at Zander and indicated Ro with a tilt of his head, "You don't want to get in her way."

Ro rolled her eyes at him, "Don't be silly."

"You're on the career track, then?" Zander asked.

Winston nodded emphatically even though Zander had directed the question towards her.

"I guess if doing what you've been hired to do means you're on the career track, then yes, I'm on the career track," she responded. She didn't want to seem like a stick in the mud, but she also didn't want them to think they could convince her to go out on the water with them when she was supposed to be getting ready for work.

"Nothing wrong with that," Zander said. Then he chuckled again, "You may find yourself disappointed with Coop."

Ro cocked her head, interested in finding out more about Cooper from wherever possible, "What do you mean?"

Zander was leaning over a scuba tank, inspecting the gages, "Coop's a great guy, I love him. But he is definitely not on the career track. He couldn't care less about business." Finding the gages to his satisfaction, Zander lifted the tank and placed it on a flat cart that he apparently used to transfer the heavy equipment to the boat. He straightened and gave her an amused smile, "Why would he worry, though, with the kind of money he's got, he doesn't have to work another day in his life."

This wasn't shocking news, but something about hearing it from a completely unbiased source made her feel...what? Excited? Nervous? She couldn't tell. She looked at Winston who seemed to be preoccupied with making adjustments to his diving mask.

Ro felt antsy. She looked out at the rising sun and thought it was probably time for her to find Carlos and Josefina and get back to the hotel.

"I'm gonna get going. I've got to get ready for work," she said.

"Thanks for walking with me," Winston said. His hair had gotten messed up with all of the scuba preparations and he still looked a little nervous. But in an adorable kind of way.

Ro smiled as she reached out and squeezed his arm, "Have fun, I'm sure it's going to be amazing."

After saying their goodbyes, Ro stepped back onto the beach. She took a deep breath of the fresh ocean air then took off towards where she'd left Carlos earlier.

There were a few more people on the beach than when they'd first arrived. Still, it was a nice walk along the water. The little tidbits Zander had provided about Cooper were mulling around in her mind. How wealthy was Cooper? What would it be like to work with someone like him? What would it be like to be with someone like him romantically? A small smile played on her lips when she let her thoughts linger there.

"Good morning!"

A man's voice brought her back to the here and now. She looked up and focused on him. It was Cooper.

Ro hesitated a moment. Was he a mirage? Had she conjured him up by thinking about him as she walked?

"Getting a little beach time before work?" He asked as he approached her. Her heart skipped a beat.

It was definitely Cooper and he was definitely real. He had on another pair of his slim fitted bathing trunks. This time they were pale blue with white cording around the waist. He wasn't shirtless, but wore a salmon colored short sleeve linen shirt, unbuttoned. He had a knack for appearing half clothed a lot of the time. Not that she was complaining.

"Hi, good morning," Ro answered, trying to focus on not staring at the way the ocean breeze made his shirt flutter open.

Cooper glanced behind her towards the dive shop in the near distance, "Did you come from Zander's?"

"Yes, I was just there."

"Going diving?" He asked.

"Oh, of course not, not today anyway. I've got so much to do to get ready for the party tonight," Ro wanted to sound both competent and convey her excitement at the upcoming party.

"Great, I'm glad you're on top of everything. Too bad you're not coming with us, though, it should be fun," Cooper said with a dimpled smile.

"Us?"

"Yeah, Zander said he's going out this morning, so I thought I'd go with. Get in some scuba time on the last day of the year."

Ro felt her jaw clench, but she managed to hold the smile on her face as she spoke, "You're going scuba diving this morning?"

"Yeah, if you didn't have so much to do you could come

with us. Maybe next time?" Cooper said as he gave her a half nod and moved past her towards the dive shop.

"Right...sure...next time," she said. With a half-hearted wave she watched Cooper turn his back and walk away. The urge to chase after him and say that she'd changed her mind was strong. Her pride, however, was stronger. She trudged back to where Carlos and Josefina were waiting. Kicking herself all the way for making such a big deal about her workload.

Her mood did not improve greatly for the rest of the day. Overrun with work, focusing hard on trying to overcome the language barrier that was ever present, and plagued with thoughts of Cooper having a great day in the sea and sun with Winston of all people, kept Ro in a sour disposition. The only thing she had to look forward to was when she finally had the time to take a bath and slip into her new dress. Then she would feel elegant. Then she would feel exotic. Then she would feel like she was starting off her new year with a brand new life.

Before that, however, she had to help at the desk and in the dining area and the adjoining ballroom, which had been opened up for the party. The ballroom wasn't quite as big as it sounded, but it was definitely luxurious and impressive enough to earn its name. The activity was non-stop and completely engaged her until just before dinner. Politely refusing Gloria's invitation to sit with her and eat, Ro excused herself to her room at half past seven to prepare for the evening.

When she entered her room she found her beautiful new red dress hanging in the small closet. She grabbed the hanger and pulled it out of the closet. Holding it up, Ro turned the gorgeous garment around, inspecting it completely to ensure nothing had happened to the delicate beadwork during the delivery process. It looked perfect. She sighed and took the dress to the full-length freestanding mirror that stood in the corner. She held the dress up against her body and her long, busy day melted away. This was going to be an amazing party and an amazing night.

After a long bath in the soaker tub, which included sumptuous jasmine and orange bath salts that were part of the spa products provided in the hotel, Ro worked on her hair. Using a set of sparkling crystal hairpins, she was able to sweep her not very long hair up. She didn't go for the sleek look, but rather a messy do with lots of bounce and wave.

She applied her eye makeup a little darker than her normal day look, it was New Year's Eve after all. The extra attention to her eye makeup paid off. Ro was impressed with how much it made the blue-grey of her eyes stand out even more than normal. Waiting to apply lipstick until after her dress was safely on, Ro went to the closet and pulled it out.

Slipping it over her head was easy. Zipping up the back was not quite as simple. She had to do a few twisting, acrobatic moves in order to get the job done. As a result her hair needed to be adjusted. Not only that, but the humidity in the air made her break out into a light sweat. Ro decided to lay on the bed under the ceiling fan to cool off. This took a long time. So long she was worried her dress was getting wrinkled.

"Well, this isn't working," she said out loud. With much care, Ro pushed herself into a sitting position then stood. She would have to get ready in the humidity and hope she didn't melt in the process.

Finally, with hair fixed, lipstick applied and a pair of strappy black high heels she was thankful she'd packed on her feet, Ro arrived at the party. Officially off the clock, she was free to take in the beautiful flower arrangements and candles that lit the long table full of delicious food from the hotel's kitchen.

Wait staff, dressed neatly in all black, some of whom she'd

worked with earlier in the day, walked the room with silver trays carrying bubbling champagne or deep red Sangria. Men in tuxedos and women in a variety of colorful cocktail dresses and evening gowns filled the space. Under the twinkling lights strung along all of the ceilings, arches and posts, the black tuxedos looked like the ocean at night and the women's dresses flashed and shimmered like tropical fish.

All of the glitzy guests were laughing and talking over the live band that were set up in the corner of the ballroom playing traditional music from Mexico. Though the rooms pulsed with excitement, all of the extra bodies in the enclosed areas made the already warm air more than Ro could handle. She wandered around the party, sipping on a glass of champagne and searching out the least hot and humid area in the whole place. This, it turned out, was the tiled area by the pool. With the lights from the party glinting off of the shining surface of the water and the roof of the courtyard open to the night sky, it was both beautiful and cooler than inside.

Ro peered into the growing crowd and searched for any familiar faces. A few of the wait staff nodded at her in greeting, but she didn't speak Spanish and they knew that, so there was no conversation. With only Spanish being spoken all around her and nobody, not Gloria or Carlos or even Alicia, nearby, Ro was feeling a little uncomfortable.

A flash of gold caught her eye through the open doorway to the crowded ballroom. She cursed her short stature when a group of partygoers passed in front of her, blocking her view. She wasn't tall enough to see over them. It might not have been Cooper. There could be a woman wearing a gold dress in the ballroom. Or a different man with a gold tuxedo jacket. Ro thought again. Never mind, that was unlikely.

Pressing forward towards the ballroom, she saw a figure

approach in her peripheral vision. A man. A tall man with solid shoulders who reached out and touched her elbow.

"Ro?"

A familiar voice, but not a gold tuxedo jacket. This jacket was black. Ro turned towards the voice and her eyes flew open.

Chapter Eight

"Winston?"

Yes, her eyes were not betraying her. It was Winston. Except better.

He held raised his arms up straight from his sides as if presenting himself for her approval. Decked out in a tuxedo, his face tanner than when she'd left him this morning, his hair styled, Winston looked taller, more sophisticated, and cuter than she'd ever seen him.

"Wow," Winston looked her up and down with appreciation, giving her a low whistle as he did. "You look amazing!"

"So do you!" She meant it, too.

"Yeah?" He flicked his lapels with his thumbs and gave her a sly smile.

Ro laughed, then asked, "Where did you get the tuxedo?"

"Your boy hooked me up."

"My boy?"

Winston tilted his head and leaned in towards her ear, "Your boy, Coop."

Ro stiffened.

"Cooper gave you that tux?"

"He lent it to me."

Eyeing Winston again, she thought she did recognize the black jacket as one of the two Cooper had held up for her inspection. With that mystery solved, the only other question she had was exactly how buddy-buddy Winston was with her new boss. She took a sip of her champagne and swallowed with pursed lips. Just as she was about to ask Winston to explain the situation, his attention shifted to something in the nearby crowd.

"There he is," Winston cupped his hand to his mouth and called out, "Coop!"

Ro turned her head just in time to see Cooper making his way through a group of party goers towards them. Her emotions ricocheted inside her like a ball in a pinball machine. Elation and excitement slammed into embarrassment and insecurity, the same kind of bashfulness she used to feel as a schoolgirl whenever she was around her crush.

Cooper looked like a movie star. The gold tuxedo jacket suited him perfectly, because he was far and away the best looking man in the room. And probably the wealthiest. As well as the owner of the hotel. Winston had been right. It was a good choice. It gave Cooper an air of being a prince, but a really cool, fashionable prince.

Cooper smiled and waved at Winston, then his gaze fell on her and he froze for a second. He looked at her intensely as if he'd just discovered a rare bird and didn't want to frighten it away. When he smiled at her it was a full-blown sexy smile, complete with a mischievous gleam in his eyes. Ro's heartbeat increased markedly. Then, still pounding, it dropped into her stomach when she saw that he had two gorgeous blonde women with him, one on each arm. They looked almost identical.

She kept her smile in place, which took every ounce of concentration she could muster. She was focusing so hard on smiling that the Barbie women went blurry and Ro could barely see Winston glancing at her out of the corner of her eye. She couldn't look at him. She knew that he must know what she was thinking, and she didn't want to risk catching his eye and falling apart right here in the middle of the party. Her focus on staying calm and pleasant made it impossible for her to speak or even to remember the names of the two women when Cooper introduced them. Not that it mattered. They were all Tamara to her.

The party went by in a blur. Ro had lost her appetite, but kept grabbing flutes full of champagne when they were offered to her, which was quite often. She lost count of how many glasses she had, the pleasant buzzing in her brain being the only thing she wanted to focus on.

Cooper flirted with her a little, told her he liked her dress, and she thought he said something about doing something together outside of work someday, maybe scuba. Or maybe she had misunderstood what he said because of the champagne.

His handsome face was in and out of her vision, as were the beautiful, perfectly made up faces of the two blondes. They ran into Gloria, who was gracious and elegant as ever. Zander showed up in the mix as well. Although she really wasn't sure if she was imagining things at that point, because she was quite tipsy. She clearly saw Alicia once, staring her down from across the room. Ro hoped that she was imagining that part of the evening.

The only thing that remained constant throughout the whole party was Winston. Even when Ro couldn't see him, she felt him standing just to the left and behind her. He offered her food and non-alcoholic drinks. He danced with her when she wanted to dance. He caught her elbow when she started to sway from too much champagne. He found her a chair when she said she was feeling tired. And he carried her high heels when she declared her feet were hot and abandoned them on the floor.

"I think maybe we should get you to bed," Winston told her when she tried to stand up, but felt dizzy and sat back down again.

Ro groaned. It was all she could do. The room was starting to spin and she was so hot she thought briefly about taking her dress off. That thought sent her into a fit of giggles.

"Yeah, I think it's bedtime for you," Winston said with amusement.

"No!" Ro shouted. A few of the partygoers near them took notice, but luckily the music and people were loud enough to mask her drunken shout from most of the room.

"C'mon, Ro, I'll walk you," Winston took her by the hands and pulled her to her feet.

"But it's not midnight yet," Ro whined. "I won't get a midnight kiss," she pushed her finger awkwardly against her lips, then started laughing again.

"I don't think you need a kiss right now," Winston said calmly as he guided her through the crowd.

"I do need a kiss," Ro argued. Her voice still too loud, "Where's Cooper?"

"Uh-oh," Winston said, picking up their pace. He was practically lifting her off of the floor to move her along more quickly.

Ro cupped her hands to her mouth the way Winston had earlier and called out, "Coop, Coop, Coop!"

More heads turned their way, but she didn't see Cooper's gold jacket anywhere.

"Whoop! Whoop! Happy New Year!" Winston called out, as if joining her in a cheer. He ducked his head down to her ear, "Come on, party girl."

He helped her out of the crowd into the gloriously cool

lobby. The tile was cold on her feet and this fascinated her. She stopped walking and stared down at her bare toes.

"My shoes!" She declared, the fact that she was bare foot just now registering.

"I've got 'em," Winston held up her black sandals for her to see. He had them dangling from two fingers.

The sight of Winston, her funny Winston, all dressed up in a tuxedo and carrying women's shoes struck Ro as the most hilarious thing she'd ever seen. She laughed so hard that she had to bend over and was afraid she would never breathe again. The laughing was so all encompassing she didn't even notice they were at her room until Winston was asking for her card key. At that point she was too drunk to argue. A little nap wouldn't hurt. She could sleep off the champagne and be back at the party in time for the midnight countdown.

She flopped face down on the bed, no longer concerned about wrinkling her brand new dress.

"Do you want some coffee or something?" Winston asked.

She mumbled into the pillow. Winston hunted around in the cabinets under her television and found some bottled water. He brought two over to the bed and placed one on the nightstand next to Ro. She turned her head so her face was barely visible.

"I need to take a nap," she said.

"Sounds like a good idea."

She rolled over so she was laying on her back and half of the bed was empty. Patting the bed next to her she said, "You can take a nap with me."

Winston hesitated.

She patted the bed harder, "Come on, buddy. I'm not gonna bite you."

"I think you need to sleep," Winston said. He looked towards the door then back at her.

"You're going to leave me on New Year's Eve?" Ro cried out in dismay.

"No, I'm not leaving," he said.

She giggled and patted the bed again, "Be my new year buddy."

He shook his head and smiled. Then he took off his jacket and hung it on the back of a chair, undid his bow tie so that it hung loose around his neck and unbuttoned the top few buttons of his shirt. He hopped up on the bed and laid back with his head propped up on the pillow next to hers.

Ro liked how Winston looked with his shirt undone and his nice, new tan. She smiled at him and he smiled back.

"You got tan today," she said, trying to act normal. It had just struck her that she and Winston had never been alone in a bedroom, let alone on a bed together.

"Yeah?" He looked at his hands and forearms for signs of a tan.

"Did you have fun scuba-ing?" She scrunched her face in confusion, trying to remember the right wording, "Or scuba...diving?"

"It was fun," he chuckled at her struggle. "It was so calm and beautiful under the surface. You should really try it."

"I will!" She smacked his arm in mock annoyance, "I've been working since I got here!"

"I know, I know."

They remained quiet for a few minutes. Ro could feel her eyelids getting heavy. She blinked hard and roused herself.

"What was Cooper like?" She asked.

"Coop?" Winston grinned at her and she smacked his arm again. He gave a little shrug, "He's a good enough guy."

"Is he?" Ro sighed dreamily.

"He's rich, that's for sure," Winston said. He stared up at the ceiling fan and mulled over his scuba diving adventure.

"For someone who has as much money as he does, he doesn't know a lot about tax shelters and investing," he added.

Ro didn't hear much of what Winston was saying, because she was lost in her own thoughts. She was thinking about Cooper being a good guy. About how he was tall, dark and handsome. How much he reminded her of...of...suddenly, tears welled up in her eyes and she started quietly crying. She sniffled and Winston looked at her.

"What's the matter?" He asked with concern, "Why are you crying?"

"You know who else was a good enough guy?" She asked. Her words slurring.

"Who?"

"Th-th-theo," Ro stammered out his name with a sob.

"Oh, no," Winston shifted so he could pull her head into the crook between his chest and shoulder. Ro pressed her face into him and had a good cry. Winston didn't say anything, he just pet the top of her head.

When she had cried herself out, Ro gave a shuddering sigh.

"Better?" Winston asked.

She nodded, but she wasn't better. She was exhausted and her head throbbed. The party was going on downstairs and she was going to miss out on all of the fun, and the midnight countdown, and on Cooper. Ro wanted to ask Winston what time it was and maybe get up and wash her face so they could go back down to the party. But instead of doing all of that, she got distracted and thought about how nice Winston smelled and how comfortable the bed felt. Then she sank into the warmth of his chest and fell asleep.

A half hour later, as the crowd downstairs counted down to midnight, Winston looked over at Ro's tear stained and mascara smeared face. She was in a deep sleep, her mouth open, a small snore escaping her nose with every breath.

"Four...three...two..." the noise of the crowd was a low murmur coming from below.

"One...Happy New Year, Ro," Winston said quietly. He carefully leaned over and kissed her on the forehead. Leaning back, he smiled at her non-response. Then he reached over to the lamp on the nightstand and turned off the light.

Chapter Nine

She was at the dentist, sitting in a large chair that was tilted so far to the back she could feel blood rushing to her head. The dentist was talking to her, but it was all incoherent mumbling because he wore a surgical mask over his face.

This was wrong. Ro wasn't due for a checkup and she certainly didn't need oral surgery.

Indignant, she tried to tell him that there must be some mistake. That's when she realized two things were keeping her from communicating with the dentist. The metal tube that sucked excess saliva during a cleaning was in her mouth. She felt her lips close around it when she tried to talk, and every time that happened the device dried up the inside of her mouth. When she tried to reach up to take the stupid thing out of her mouth, she realized that she was strapped down in the chair. Not only could she not move her arms, but she couldn't get out of the chair at all.

Panic filled her, making her arms and hands feel like pins pricked along her skin. Ro's eyes widened as the dentist moved closer to her, murmuring behind his mask, adjusting the glaring light above her head so that it shone right into her eyes. She tried to close them, but the light somehow held them open. A sharp pain shot through her head, blinding her.

She woke with a start.

"Too much?" A familiar voice asked.

Ro tried to blink, but her face was squished into a pillow. She had to move her head in order to see anything, but when she did, a stabbing pain shot from her forehead to her temples to the back of her brain, making her groan.

"I'll close them," the voice said.

She heard a squeaky grinding sound that echoed in her ears, making her wince. The blinds. The voice was closing the blinds on her windows.

"Shh..." she tried to say, but her mouth was so dry she couldn't make the sound. Sucking in her breath to steel herself against the pain, Ro unburied her face from her pillow and turned her head so she was looking into the shadowed room. Then she lowered her head gently back down to rest on the pillow again, working her tongue around in her mouth as she did to try and build up enough saliva to speak.

"I brought you some coffee," the voice said. It was Winston. She could see that now in the dim light. He was sitting back down into a chair that he'd pulled up to her nightstand. Ro squinted because even the grey light of the room was too much for her tender eyeballs. There was a coffee carafe, cream and sugar, and a gleaming white cup waiting for her on her nightstand. He held his own steaming cup in his lap.

A jolt of fear went through her powerless body. Was she late for work?

"What time is it?" She croaked.

"It's just after nine," he answered, taking a sip of his coffee.

"Oh no!" She started to push herself up from the bed, but

was forced back down by the splitting pain in her head combined with a horrible queasiness in her stomach.

"It's Saturday," Winston reassured her. "You don't have work today. I double checked with that Gloria lady."

Relief flooded her, but was quickly replaced with dismay as the details of the night before became clearer in her mind.

"What did I do?" She groaned.

"In general? Or do you want specifics?"

"I hate champagne," she complained.

Winston grinned, "You could have fooled me."

"Oh God," Ro lifted her hand to her forehead and tried to rub the pain out of it. Her stomach roiled.

"I got you some ibuprofen," he leaned forward and poured coffee into her cup, adding cream. "Carlos is sending up a big, greasy breakfast with some kind of jalapeño or Chile pepper stuff he wants you to eat. Says it'll make you feel better."

The thought of food sent her stomach into another tail-spin. She groaned again, shoving her face back into the pillow.

Winston chuckled, "Happy New Year, Ro!"

"No."

"C'mon, it's your first day off, and the first day of the year!"

"Do over," she mumbled. The hangover was bad enough, although she knew she would get over it...eventually. What Ro couldn't stop thinking about was what a drunken fool she'd been the night before. What did Cooper think of her now? And Alicia? She could lose her job.

Some of it was a blur, but she did remember Winston removing her from the party and bringing her to her room. She didn't remember a whole lot after that. He had been laying next to her on the bed. Then what happened? She gasped, jerking up to her elbows and looking down to see what she was wearing. She was still in her red dress, though it was rumpled and twisted around her thighs. She looked at Winston with wide-open eyes.

"Did we...?" She didn't know how to say what she was thinking.

She looked him up and down, his feet were bare under his trousers, his shirt was completely undone, as if it had been off then put back on again.

He creased his brow, wondering why she was flipping out. Then it hit him.

"No, we didn't do anything. We slept," he said.

"Oh, thank God," she flopped back down with relief.

"You don't have to be so happy about it," he said with mock indignation. He thrust his shoulders back and puffed up his chest, "I don't want to brag, but if we had done anything you'd remember."

"Oh, be quiet."

"Just sayin'," he cocked his head at her and took another drink of his coffee.

Ro decided to push herself into a sitting position and try to swallow the ibuprofen with some coffee. Winston watched her wobble around until she was sitting with her legs dangling off the side of the bed, her face screwed up with the pain and nausea of it all. He handed her two pills and her coffee.

"Why are you here now?" She asked, taking the pills and coffee from him.

He scoffed, "I'm taking care of you, you drunken mess."

She choked back a laugh, almost snorting the coffee out of her nose. A fresh sea of pain washed through her forehead, making her wince.

"I thought you might need some help getting ready," he continued.

She looked at him, confused, "For what?"

"We've been invited to go to the ruins."

She took another sip of coffee. It was hot and delicious and she hoped it would help her feel better, but she couldn't imagine being well enough to leave her room today. Let alone go on a day trip to the Mayan ruins.

Winston eyed her reaction and must have deduced that she wasn't thrilled with the idea. He leaned back in his chair and put his feet up on the bed next to her like he always did when he was feeling cocky. He knew something she didn't.

"What?" She asked.

"You don't want to go?"

"I will be lucky if I make it out of this bed today."

His eyes twinkled with amusement. Like a naughty little kid who's pulling a prank.

"What?" She asked, exasperated.

"Coop invited us to go to the ruins today," he annunciated Cooper's nickname so she was sure to understand.

Ro's heart leapt even as she was irked at Winston's teasing. Nerves sprung up in her already unstable stomach and she didn't know if she was going to laugh or cry or vomit.

Winston sighed, taking his feet off of the bed and the cup from her hands, which were trembling. He placed both of their cups on the nightstand. Leaning forward with his elbows on his knees, he took her hands in his. He looked into her eyes with affection, then squeezed her hands gently and said, "I know, I know...you changed your mind."

With Winston's support, Ro was ready for their day outing in less than two hours. He made her promise that she would drink water almost continually while they were out in the heat of the day.

"Dehydration is your enemy," he told her as he packed several bottles of water into a day pack for her and even more into his larger pack. Ro nodded in mute submission. She was depending on the fact that Winston was not a hot mess to get her through this day.

Her hangover had reduced to what felt like a thin film of glass covering her skin, which any wrong move could crack and send shattering to the ground. Still, she was dressed for the day with comfortable shorts, light hiking shoes, a white tank top with a thin, blue cotton button up shirt over top, a straw hat Winston insisted on buying her at the hotel shop, and sunglasses. She was up and moving, looked reasonably cute, and was determined to spend the day doing something cultural and fun. Something with Cooper.

Cooper, on the other hand, was cool, sexy and in control as he met them in the lobby. One of the two blondes was still on his arm. No explanation of where the other blonde had went.

"One down and one to go," Ro said under her breath as she climbed into the stretch SUV Cooper had called to take them to Chichén Itzá.

It was over a two-hour drive to the site of the ancient ruins. The vehicle was air conditioned, stocked with food and drinks, decked out with a killer sound system, and an absolute misery for Ro.

The floating sensation caused by being in the back end of a stretch vehicle only exacerbated her queasiness and she was practically green for the full two-hour ride. Cooper and Winston talked and laughed about topics Ro couldn't focus on. It turned out the blonde's name was Tomi. Her name fit her bleached hair, deep tan, heavy lipstick, skimpy tank top look. Tomi kept her oversized sunglasses on and was pretty standoffish, which was fine. Ro had little interest in knowing about her competition, even if she hadn't been hung over.

The ruins were amazing. Ro regained some of her energy in the fresh air as they made their way around the different sections of the site. Cooper had hired a tour guide named Paco to take them around and explain what they were seeing. Paco was funny and interesting. When he said her name, he rolled his tongue when pronouncing the 'r', making 'Señorita Ro' sounded more like 'Señorita R-r-ro'. Her name had heft when Paco said it and she liked that. Winston kept her supplied with bottles of water and, despite the heat and humidity, she felt like she was getting back to normal.

The Temple of Kulkulcan dominated the site. A massive pyramid structure that rose 80 feet into the sky. It had four sides, each equipped with narrow stone steps that led to the platform on top. Cooper and Winston wanted to climb the steps to the top. Tomi was bored with the idea, but Ro thought she could accompany them.

The steps were narrow and steep, and there was no handrail. Apparently ancient Mayans didn't build their stairways with modern codes in mind. After trying the first few steps, Ro felt dizzy and a little sick again. She decided to sit it out this time and instead stood at the foot of the stairway next to a huge snake head carved of stone, watching the two men climb.

When they reached the top Ro saw them high five each other. They waved to her and Tomi. She waved back and glanced sideways at Tomi, who didn't wave at all. Ro wondered if her own personality was too enthusiastic for Cooper's tastes. If Tomi was an indication of the kind of woman he liked, Ro might have to tone her naturally nice persona down a few notches to get him to notice her.

After soaking in as much mind blowing architectural accomplishment and ancient Mayan lifestyle stories they could in just a few hours, Cooper decided they should head out. He wanted to stop at one of his favorite restaurants in Tulum on the way back for a meal. As much as Ro was impressed with the ruins and enjoyed Paco's tour guide skills, she was thankful to climb back into the air-conditioned car. Knowing that she could revisit this site in the future whenever she desired helped her feel better about not being completely herself on her first visit.

The outing must have taken more out of her than she'd realized, or maybe it was the humming engine of the car, because on the drive to Tulum she dozed off. What was going to be another two hour ride where she might feel well enough and finally have time to chat with Cooper, turned into less than 20 minutes of awake time. Plus she had the added humiliation of having fallen asleep like a child while Tomi had, presumably, stayed wide awake, all blonde and busty.

"You have to try the grilled octopus," Cooper was saying to Winston as Ro blinked her eyes open.

"I don't know about octopus," Winston grimaced.

"You're joining the party!" Cooper smiled at Ro as she straightened up and tried to pretend she hadn't been slumped in the corner of her seat, probably snoring.

"How are you feeling?" Winston asked. He reached for his bag where she knew more bottles of water waited.

She shook her head at him, indicating she didn't want any water right now. She couldn't think about drinking anything at the moment, in fact. Her bladder was about to burst.

"I'm fine," she said. "And, yes," she gave Cooper the best smile she could muster, "I am ready for the party!"

The party, it turned out, was at Rosa Negra. An eco-chic, Latin restaurant and bar located on the main beach strip in Tulum. Despite the simple dirt road it sat on, Rosa Negra was a nice restaurant, very nice in fact. Ro knew immediately when they walked in that they were too dusty and casually dressed to justify the warm welcome they received. The manager approached with an ear-to-ear smile, shook Cooper's hand and showed them to a table with a fine view of the wide room. It was easy to be impressed by the reaction Cooper got wherever he went. He was well known and, it appeared, well liked.

The walls of Rosa Negra were made of rough, white stone. Finely woven baskets acted as hanging light fixture covers. They were strung from a ceiling made up of single sticks pushed tightly together like floor mats. This rustic edge was in contrast to the fine china and glassware that graced the tables and the funky lounge, almost disco, music that mingled with conversations of well-dressed patrons.

Ro excused herself to the ladies room. Tomi didn't join her, which was a clear sign that they were not friendly. Not that Ro needed more proof of the other woman's disinterest. Tomi was obviously into Cooper and nobody else. In some ways, Ro could completely understand.

After she took care of bathroom business, Ro splashed water in her face and dried it with the paper towels provided. She dug through her purse to find the small brush and makeup bag and took a few minutes to spruce up for dinner. At least she looked better than she had this morning. When she returned to the table the waiter, Hector, was placing wild looking drinks at each seat, including hers.

Slices of cucumber and lemon mixed with a clear liquid inside of a long stemmed wine glass. Wisps of what looked like smoke, but must have been caused by dry ice, filled the top of the glass and spilled over the side. Hector pulled out her chair with a flourish. Ro thanked him and took her seat, inspecting her cocktail.

"What are these?" She asked.

"Gin and tonic...basically," Winston said, lifting his to his mouth and blowing the smoky steam towards her. Ro laughed.

"To the first day of the rest of our lives," Cooper said, raising his drink up in a toast. They all clinked glasses and even Tomi cracked a smile.

From there, the evening got even better.

To say the food was remarkable would not have done the

chef, or the staff, at Rosa Negra justice. The presentation was enough to rocket this place into the most impressive restaurant Ro had ever entered. Truffle popovers, roasted corn with butter and chile powder served on skewers, tuna sashimi, Kobe beef steak, seafood salad, and grilled octopus, as Cooper had suggested.

Her appetite had returned with a vengeance just in time, as the portions were huge and everything was delicious. The octopus was served in tact, artfully presented in the center of the plate so that the tentacled arms appeared to be climbing towards the ceiling. When Hector placed Winston's in front of him, Winston grimaced at the sight.

Cooper laughed at his reaction, "Don't knock it till you've tried it!"

Winston made a stoic face and picked up his knife and fork, which made Cooper laugh again. He looked at Ro and jerked his thumb at Winston, "You've got your hands full with this one."

Ro's face went numb. Though she managed to hold onto her amused expression, inside she felt a rising sense of dread. What did Cooper mean by that comment? She shot Winston a look, but he was busy making faces while trying to cut up his octopus. Entertaining both Cooper and Tomi, who were charmed with him.

Ro's mind tumbled over the details of the past 24 hours. Winston hanging around her at the New Year's Eve party. Winston taking her up to her room. The fact that he'd specifically said, "*We've* been invited to go to the ruins." We? There was no *we*. But Cooper didn't know that. He thought she and Winston were together. An item. Dating.

She looked around the table. Tomi, gorgeous, silently sipping her third drink of the night. Winston chewing his first bite of grilled octopus and making jokes. Cooper slapping Winston's back and giving Ro a friendly smile, as if they were bonding through their mutual relationships with Winston.

The reality of her situation sunk in. This was a date.

Heat rose in her cheeks as the implications of the misunderstanding became clear. She and Winston were on a double date with Cooper and Tomi.

Cooper didn't like her romantically. Winston was undermining her attempts at a brand new life. She was nothing more than a dreamy eyed secretary with a huge crush on her boss.

Their dinner ended with a fantastic dessert. A huge chocolate sphere with a creamy filling. Hector poured hot caramel over the top of the sphere to melt through the chocolate so they could all dig in with their spoons. The sphere was large enough for all four of them to share. Ro barely ate a bite.

Chapter Ten

By Monday morning, Ro had determined an appropriate course of action to get her new life back on track.

First, she had to avoid Winston. That was clear. She couldn't have Cooper and the rest of the people in her new surroundings believe that anything other than friendship was going on between her and Winston. She figured she could just stay busy for the rest of the time he was in Mexico on vacation. Once he flew home it would be easy to put him firmly away in her past and move freely into her future.

She'd already successfully kept away from him all day Sunday. Feigning the need to recuperate from her hangover and their day trip, Ro had spent her Sunday off in her room, plotting and catching up on sleep. Besides a few texts in the morning checking in to make sure she was okay, Winston had left her alone.

The second thing she decided she needed to do was put herself in Cooper's path as much as possible. Ironically, being his secretary didn't equate with seeing him much during the day. His tendency to take off on adventures was something she must learn to take advantage of if she ever wanted him to see her as anything except his employee. Taking care of her administrative duties could be done quietly and efficiently so that the next time Cooper brought up doing something like scuba diving, Ro would jump on the invitation.

This realization led directly to the third task in her plan to create her brand new life. Ro determined that she must be as open and friendly, even flirtatious, with Cooper as possible. This change was more subtle and something she was going to have to concentrate on to accomplish. No moment between them could be lost to insecurity or the formalities of their working relationship. If Ro wanted to be with Cooper in her new life, she must make her desires clear.

At nine o'clock Monday morning she walked the short distance from her room to her office, ready to take on this new day of the new year in her new life with gusto. She had opted out of a morning walk on the beach with Carlos and Josefina today, afraid they might run into Winston.

Instead, Ro spent some extra time getting dressed. A pale blue cotton dress she had previously determined was too short for work, now seemed like the perfect choice. Tanned from her day at the ruins, Ro saw that the dress not only clung nicely, but showed off the blue in her eyes against her darker skin tone.

Making sure her hair was artfully tousled, she went to the dining room and grabbed a quick breakfast to take back to her room. She didn't want to run into Winston while she was eating. He hadn't texted her or shown up at her hotel room this morning. Hopefully he was off on some tourist adventure and would stay away all day.

Not surprisingly, Cooper didn't show his face at nine o'clock. Ro busied herself checking emails, reviewing his business schedule, which was pretty sparse, and opening the mail. She popped in to see Gloria mid-morning and did some filing and mail opening for her as well. Ro returned to her office to find the whole place dead silent. She was beginning to wonder if Cooper was even in his rooms and glanced at the closed double doors continually, waiting for a sign of him. The determination to enjoy her day was beginning to wane as the hours passed with no Cooper in sight.

Just before lunch, the slim desk phone that had sat quietly on her desk since she started this job last week, buzzed. Someone was calling and Ro froze for a second, not sure how she should answer the phone. She cleared her throat and picked up the receiver.

"Good morning, Cooper Rivera's office. How may I help you?"

"Nice greeting! You're a real professional."

"Cooper?"

"Yes, it's me. I have something I want you to see," he said.

Ro turned towards the double doors, "Do you want me to come into your office?"

Cooper laughed with gusto, "No, come to the dock."

"The dock?"

"Yes, by Zander's dive shop. You know where that is?"

"I do," she answered. She stood up, her nerves and excitement taking over, "Right now?"

"Yes, come now. The day is wasting away!"

Without another word, the call was disconnected. Ro placed the receiver back into its slim receptacle and smiled to herself. Standing up, she smoothed her dress. She hadn't expected her next opportunity to be with Cooper outside of the office to come so quickly. But she truly felt like she was ready.

Almost 20 minutes later Ro approached the dock by Zander's dive shop. Her stroll down the beach had been hotter than she anticipated. Every other time she'd been on the beach it had been early morning and not nearly as crowded as it was now.

As Ro picked her way through tourists sitting on blankets or under oversized beach umbrellas or playing Frisbee along the water's edge, she felt a bit uptight. Like Mary Poppins trying to walk across the fine, white sand, without getting it in her shoes or stuck in between her toes. Families and college students and lovebirds all romped around her in their swimming suits. She remained formal and stiff while everyone else played.

She tried to relax and remember that she was on a beautiful tropical beach, on her way to meeting her handsome, single boss who wanted her to join him. This could turn into the fun, flirty and intimate moment she'd been dreaming about. Briefly, she wondered if Tomi was going to be with him. Then she wondered if Tomi would be wearing a gorgeous revealing swimsuit, while she was stuck in her short, but comparatively conservative, blue dress.

As she got closer she saw that Zander was talking to a man wearing a white hat who stood on an impressive yacht that was tied to the dock. Ro looked around for any sign of Cooper. Zander spied her and gave her a full arm wave, motioning for her to come over. The man on the yacht turned to see who had Zander's attention, and the instant she saw who it was, her heart lifted.

Cooper.

His gorgeous face broke into a wide smile. He was beautiful. A tan over his already dark toned skin. A tight fitting polo shirt in variegated black and white stripes. One of his signature slim fitted swimming trunks, these in black, showing off his incredible physique. The white boating hat sitting jauntily on his head.

"Ro!" He waved at her from high atop the shining boat and Ro felt a thrill flip through her stomach.

This was incredible. Were they taking a yacht out onto the water? Throwing a party? She waved as her steps quickened as her excitement grew, imagining all of the possibilities. The bright turquoise water lapped against the clean, smooth white hull. Stunning. Her concerns about being too prim as she had walked through the crowds of tourists on the beach disappeared. Her dress was perfect for a yacht party.

Ro stepped onto the dock and noticed another person who had emerged out of nowhere to stand next to Cooper. Her toe hit a plank of wood that stuck up unexpectedly and she tripped forward, catching herself with the handrail.

"Whoa," Zander exclaimed and trotted over to offer her a hand. "Watch your step," he said.

Ro took his hand and steadied herself before looking back towards Cooper waiting on the boat. Maybe she had been seeing things and the person standing next to Cooper was not who she thought it was. Zander led her towards the yacht and Ro cringed.

Nope. She hadn't been seeing things. It was Winston's face she saw next to Cooper's on the yacht. Winston's grinning face.

Ro was speechless as the two men waved to her, which was probably a good thing. If she'd been able to say anything she may have had a few choice words for her old office buddy. What in the world was he doing here? On Cooper's yacht?

"It's a beauty, isn't it?" Zander asked. He thought she was astounded at the sight of the yacht, not who was on it.

Ro nodded mutely.

"Come aboard!" Cooper called happily to her as Zander showed her to the portable steps that stretched up from the dock and across to the deck. "You coming, Zander?" He asked the Aussie.

Zander shook his head, his blonde dreadlocks bouncing, "Not today, mate. I've got clients."

"Fair enough, another time?" Cooper asked. Zander said something she didn't quite catch. As she made her way up and over the steps, Cooper was distracted talking to Zander over the edge of the yacht.

Winston took Ro's hand as she reached the end of the steps to ensure she transferred onto the deck safely. She almost swatted his hand away, but felt a little unstable and was forced to take it to steady herself.

Winston had on a pair of long, white shorts and a loose fitting royal blue cotton shirt that hung casually past his waist. He, too, was nicely tan and if she wasn't so furious at him she would tell him that he looked good. Vacations suited him.

"What are you doing here?" She hissed at him.

His eyebrows raised in amusement at her tone. Before he had a chance to react, Cooper turned towards them.

"What do you think?" Cooper asked, spreading his arms wide to indicate the yacht.

Ro didn't know what to say.

"This guy," Cooper stepped to Winston and put one hand on his shoulder and one on his arm, pushing him back and forth like a big brother teasing a little brother. Like they were friends. "This guy is a genius!"

Ro looked at Winston then Cooper, not understanding.

"Not genius, really," Winston said humbly.

"What did he do?" Ro asked.

"He convinced me to buy this..." again, Cooper stretched his arms out like a game show host showing off the grand prize to a contestant, "...as a tax write off!" Cooper let go a great hoot of laughter, then slapped Winston on the back as he walked past him towards the bow railing.

Ro's mouth dropped open. She stared at Winston, in shock.

"We've been yacht shopping," Winston said quietly to her.

She smacked his arm, "What are you doing? He can't write this off...can he?"

He shrugged, "Actually, he can if he uses it for hotel events."

"Want a drink?" Cooper pulled open the door of a small fridge built into the bench seating at the bow. "Then we'll give you a tour."

Ro took the drink. She needed something to help manage her disappointment. Not that the yacht wasn't beautiful. It was splendid, with polished wood decks and handrails, a spacious cabin with a large living room and bedrooms, or berths, enough to sleep over a dozen people. A captain and small crew were there to handle the actual sailing and there was a chef and staff to cook for them and clean up afterwards. No, it wasn't the yacht that disappointed her.

It was Winston.

The way he kept sitting by her, looking at her. The way Cooper joked with him constantly. The way he had somehow infiltrated her new world and was having a better time than she was in it.

All of this was annoying. And disappointing. Then annoying again.

Ro sat gloomily on the white sectional couch that stretched around what Cooper had called the saloon. She thought it seemed more like the living room. She'd abandoned Winston and Cooper at the helm with the Captain. They were involved in looking at the controls and other gadgets that held no interest for Ro. The Captain was a middle-aged man with dirty blonde hair, a hard jawline, and intelligent eyes. He seemed competent, which was all Ro cared about.

To her surprise, Tomi entered the room from the door that led down to the sleeping areas. She wore a red bikini and her sunglasses, nothing else. She didn't speak to Ro, just went to the long, mirrored bar that filled most of the inside wall and pulled out two glasses.

"Hi, Tomi," Ro said, giving the other woman a small wave from the couch. Maybe she hadn't seen her when she came in.

Tomi turned her head towards Ro and smirked.

"I'm not Tomi," the blonde said.

Just then another bikini clad blonde emerged from the bowels of the yacht. Ro blinked. This one's bikini was black, but she was also wearing a pair of sunglasses and, to Ro's confusion, this one was also Tomi.

"Hi," the black bikini blonde said to Ro. Then added, "I didn't know you were here."

"Tomi?" Ro asked.

The blondes looked at each other and giggled. Black bikini threw her arm around red bikini and said, "Tara, this is Ro. Ro, this is my sister, Tara."

Twins. How had she totally forgotten seeing them together at the party?

A rush of disgust swept through Ro. Was Cooper actually dating twins? Like some kind of Hugh Hefner wannabe?

"When did you come onboard?" Tomi asked. She took the drink Tara had fixed at the bar and joined Ro on the couch.

"Just a little while ago," Ro answered. Flustered at their presence and what it meant, Ro fought the urge to make a dash for the door.

"Want anything to drink?" Tara asked.

"No, thanks," Ro lifted her not yet finished bottle of ginger beer that Cooper had given her earlier.

Tara plopped her barely covered rear end down on the opposite side of the couch. Ro was flanked by two blondes on a Austin Powers style couch in the saloon of a yacht in the Caribbean. At the very least, she realized, over the past week her life had become surreal.

"So, you're the girl dating Winston?" Tara asked.

"What? No, absolutely not," Ro responded.

Tomi furrowed her brow, "But, I thought–"

"I know! Everyone thinks we're dating, but we're not," Ro felt somewhat relieved at the chance to announce the truth.

Tomi and Tara exchanged a look.

"So he's single," Tara said. Ro could barely see her blonde eyebrows raise with interest behind those giant, crystal studded sunglasses.

"Yes," Ro answered. Her thoughts flew over the past five years searching for a moment when Winston had ever announced he had a girlfriend. She couldn't even think of a time when he said he'd been dating anyone. At least not seriously.

"So he's fair game?" Tara asked.

"Fair game?" Ro didn't quite understand.

"He's single, you're not dating him. So he's fair game?"

Ro was so surprised at the question, she couldn't give a straight answer. All she said was, "Winston?"

Tara and Tomi both giggled again.

"He's hot," Tara said.

Before Ro could think of an appropriate response, Cooper and Winston appeared in the windows. There were windows spread across the entire length of the saloon that looked out over the bow of the boat and across the bright blue ocean. The men were making their way down the stairway from the helm, laughing and talking. Cooper knocked on the window when he saw the three women on the couch.

"We're setting sail!" He declared, his voice muted through the glass.

Both of the twins lifted their drinks in a toast towards him. Ro stiffened. They were sailing? Into the ocean? The men entered the room. Cooper was beaming as he jogged towards the couch and sat down next to Tomi, putting his arm around her shoulders in a proprietary way. Winston, a little less boisterous, took a seat between Ro and Tara. Ro gave him a look of alarm.

"We're just taking it for a spin and eating dinner on the deck," he explained. He noticed her expression and asked, "Are you okay with that? Do you want to stay here?"

"Why would she want to stay behind?" Cooper corrected Winston. So sure of the appeal of his yacht outing, he was unable to entertain Winston's comment.

The motors that lay somewhere below them in an unseen place, kicked into life. A powerful humming sent a low-grade vibration through the floor, the couch, and Ro's body. Tomi and Tara giggled at the sensation.

"It's just dinner on the water, then we're coming back," Winston spoke quietly to her so the others couldn't hear. He was still concerned, she could tell. He looked out the windows as two of the crew appeared outside. He gave her a reassuring smile, "But if you want to stay here you better say something before we pull away from the dock. I don't know how long it takes to turn these things around."

Ro stood up quickly. Without looking at Winston or responding to what he'd just said, without making eye contact with anyone, she made her way to the door and left the cabin.

Chapter Eleven

It was warm outside. The slow, humid warmth of the tropics. But the breeze off of the ocean was refreshing, and the view was enough to take her breath away.

Floating directly on top of the crystal clear water made it seem like she was actually standing inside of a postcard, surrounded by the ocean that stretched, uninterrupted, to the horizon. Low waves reflected the sunlight like a million diamonds twinkling on top the brilliant blue water. The sky was mostly clear, with just a few white puffy clouds perfecting the picture.

Ro leaned against the railing, looking into the distance. The yacht undulated with the waves, creating a rolling sensation. Combined with the rumble of the engines below, it was hypnotic.

Winston appeared at her side. He leaned on the railing next to her so their elbows were touching, and joined her in looking out over the water.

"You okay?" He asked.

For the 15 or so minutes it had taken them to leave the dock and maneuver through the other boats and obstacles close to shore, Ro had stood alone at the bow. The fresh air and breeze on her cheeks helped clear her muddled thoughts.

"I'm okay," she answered, though she didn't look at him.

"This is crazy, isn't it?" Winston said with a laugh of disbelief.

Ro didn't answer. She kept her eyes trained on the sparkling water and the distant horizon. A minute went by and Winston cleared his throat. Ro continued staring at the horizon. Hard.

He tried again, "I guess you could tell that Coop and Tomi are a thing?"

"Are they?" Ro pursed her lips.

"Yeah, I think so. That's how they act anyway."

Winston turned towards her, leaning sideways against the railing. She was curious if Cooper was also dating Tomi's twin, but didn't want to talk to Winston about any of it. She didn't want to talk to Winston at all.

"Look, Ro, I'm sure you're disappointed. But honestly," he leaned towards her and lowered his voice, "I don't think you're missing out on a whole lot. I mean, Coop is nice and everything, but he can be a little..." he searched for the word.

Ro turned her gaze on him, "A little what?"

He shrugged and looked away. Uncomfortable under her stare.

"You know," he said, giving her a sideways glance.

"No, Winston, I don't know," she retorted. "I don't know much about Cooper or his relationships, because you are the one that is spending every moment of every day with him. Not me."

She turned back to glare at the ocean.

Winston let out a laugh that was more of a snort and asked, "What?"

When she didn't answer, he looked around where they stood, as if searching for the answer in the teak decking or the gleaming white sides of the cabin. Then he let out a frustrated sigh. Ro shot him a look. What did he have to be frustrated about?

"You know what you're doing, don't you?" Winston asked, all humor gone from his voice.

"What do you think I'm doing?"

"You're doing it all over again."

"Doing what all over again?"

"Theo," he said, locking eyes with her. "You're doing exactly what you did with Theo, and with a man who seems to be a lot like Theo," he gestured towards the cabin, but kept his eyes on her.

Ro sucked in her breath and held it. She didn't know if she was going to cry or yell, so she kept her lips clamped together. Winston shook his head and raked his hand through his hair. He let out an empty laugh.

"It's like you can't see past their show. You get all wrapped up in some fantasy of who they are and you can't see the truth," he said.

Anger bubbled inside of her. She glanced self-consciously at the cabin windows. Her cheeks and eyes were hot with emotion, and she worried those inside were watching.

"What are you talking about? What truth?" She hissed at him.

"That men like Theo, men like Coop, are always going to go for the Tamara's and Tomi's of the world. And that's fine, that's great! Let them have each other, I say. Except you think that means you're not worth anything," Winston had moved closer to her and was speaking low. His big, brown eyes looked deeply into hers and her stomach clenched with the intensity. There was something in his eyes that she couldn't name, a question, like he was pleading with her. His voice dropped even lower, rumbling up from his chest, "They don't see you because they're not looking. And that's their fault, not yours. You deserve someone who treats you like a queen, not an after thought."

With that, Winston left and the angry knot in Ro's stomach twisted into despair. It took everything in her not to burst into tears. Her eyes welled up and she turned into the wind, breathing fast to try and regain control. Ro stayed where she was as the yacht moved further and further away from land. Pretending to be enjoying the view until her urge to cry disappeared.

❧

DINNER WAS AMAZING. The table was set up on an outside deck under the stars. The furniture and table dressings were the utmost in luxury with fine china, crystal glasses, and heavy silver tableware. This stately service seemed even more extravagant out in the open water. As if the power and money that brought it here had dominion over the very sea upon which they floated.

They had lobster, of course. What else would you have for dinner on a lavish yacht? They also had wine, lots of wine. Ro didn't partake. She was already experiencing a roller coaster of emotions, wine would only exacerbate her problems.

Winston drank. As did Cooper and the twins, who had changed into evening wear for dinner. Tomi wore a skimpy black dress and black stilettos. Ro thought this was silly and rather dangerous, considering how much Tomi was drinking. She could easily trip in those heels and topple over the railing if she wasn't careful.

Tara wore an even skimpier dress than her sister. Red, go figure. And she made sure to sit next to Winston at the table so she could laugh at his jokes, touch his arm whenever possible, and act basically like she was in heat. Of course, this was just Ro's personal opinion. She didn't share it with anyone.

She did her best to enjoy the dinner, even if by the end of it she was feeling like a third, no, make that a fifth wheel.

Afterwards they retired to the saloon at Cooper's insistence. Ro would have rather stayed on deck and looked at the stars and the deep, black ocean around them. But it was Cooper's party and he had something he wanted to show them all.

"Look what came with the yacht!" Cooper reached into a small cabinet behind the bar area and pulled out two microphones.

"Is that...?" Tara giggled and took one of them, holding it up to her mouth.

"Hang on," Cooper said, ducking behind the bar.

The flat screen TV that was mounted on the wall lit up. A bright purple background with plain white text in all caps read, "KARAOKE NIGHT".

Tomi and Tara squealed with delight as Tomi grabbed the other microphone. Cooper presented them all with a printout of the songs available on the machine. Ro groaned internally. Without the benefit of alcohol, she expected karaoke to be an excruciating experience.

She glanced at Winston. He was perusing the list of songs. He hadn't really engaged with her since their conversation on the bow. Drinking steadily all evening had made him funnier than normal, but most of that good humor had been directed towards Cooper and, to her surprised annoyance, towards Tara. Winston always gave Ro his full attention when they were together. But not tonight. She wished she could share her discontent with him and let him make her feel better, like he always did.

Ro went to the bar and grabbed one of the open bottles of wine. A nice Chenin Blanc. She needed a little something to relax during this evening's entertainment.

"Oh, good, you're trying it," Cooper said. He had joined

her, leaning both elbows on the bar and bending his head down so his eyes were even with hers. His breath smelled like alcohol and he was a little unsteady on his feet. Even drunk, Cooper was astonishingly attractive. Dark hair sexily messed up, eyes glinting with mischief, giving a hint of the unexpected, his voice deep and gravelly. He nodded towards the bottle, "You'll have to tell me if you like it."

"I will," she answered as she finished pouring a generous amount into a large wine glass, trying not to blush under his sudden attention.

"Let's get this show on the road!" Winston called out from the couch where Tara had settled in right next to him, or vice versa.

Tomi and Tara sang the first song, "We Are Family", an expected cliché. Then they pranced around to "Call Me Maybe". They convinced Cooper to go next. He chose "Do Ya Think I'm Sexy" by Rod Stewart. His performance was hard to witness. Ro stole a few glances towards Winston while Cooper sang slightly off key, gyrating his hips and pointing occasionally at an overly receptive Tomi. Ro was certain Winston would be thinking the same thing she was, that this was like being trapped in a horrible, tacky nightmare. She didn't catch his eye, because he was laughing with Tara and Tomi. For the first time in their years of friendship, Ro felt ignored. It wasn't a good feeling.

Cooper offered her the microphone when he was done, and she politely declined.

"I haven't picked a song yet," she said with a dry laugh. Hopefully they would be entertained enough with each other throughout the night so she could stay on the couch and out of the spotlight.

Tomi took the stage next with a not too bad, for a drunk girl, version of "Can't Help Falling in Love". Although, her overuse of pouty lips and Marilyn Monroe-like antics was cringe worthy. Then Cooper and the twins started "Sweet Home Alabama". They pulled a reluctant Winston up to sing with them while Ro smiled and clapped. Her plan to escape having to sing included being the perfect audience. It was no fun to sing karaoke to an empty room.

Next, Cooper turned on "Margaritaville", insisting the others stay and sing with him, aiming all of their talents towards Ro on the couch. Weren't they almost back to shore? Ro smiled and clapped at the appropriate moments, wondering the whole time exactly how much longer this evening was going to last.

Finally the song was over and Cooper and the girls tumbled, laughing, onto the couch. Cooper raised his hand as a high five to Ro and she smacked it with her palm. Her false enthusiasm seemed to be working.

"Your turn," Cooper said to her, offering her the microphone.

Ro opened her mouth to refuse, but couldn't think of anything to say. At this point refusing could be taken as an insult, after the others had all gone along with the fun. At the very least she would seem to be a real stick in the mud, as her mother used to say. Ro's throat went dry. Nerves.

"I'll go," Winston interrupted. He deftly took the microphone from Cooper's outstretched hand and went to the karaoke controls, punching a few buttons. The title "How am I Supposed to Live Without You" by Michael Bolton appeared on the screen. Tara gave a drunken squeal and clapped her hands together while Winston positioned himself center stage in front of the couch.

He had sensed her embarrassment and thrown himself on the grenade, as it were. Ro watched him, grateful to be saved.

The blue in his shirt looked good against his tan. He had rolled the long sleeves up on the cotton shirt and his forearm flexed as he lifted the microphone. Winston had a nice, muscular build. She hadn't always noticed this fact, but since he'd been in Playa del Carmen his masculinity seemed to have escalated. His hair looked good today, too. Windblown and messy, and somehow sexier than his normal put together look.

Something in the look on his face caught her attention. As he waited for the light, tinkling intro to play, his stance had the same appeal she'd seen in singers at rock concerts. She got the feeling that he was no stranger to performing. He kept his eyes trained on the floor in front of him, waiting for the lyrics to begin. When they did he didn't need to look at the TV screen to follow along. Winston knew all the words. Winston, it turned out, knew how to sing.

With the very first words of the song, "I could hardly believe it...", his voice captured her. Every bit as good as Michael Bolton, maybe even better. Winston's singing voice was smoky, which gave the lyrics an edgier feel. Cooper and the twins were just as drawn into his performance as Ro was from the moment he began. Each word carried a wealth of emotion as Winston put everything he was into this song. When he got to the chorus, his face twisted with focus and passion and he belted out, "How am I supposed to live without you..." As he sang he lifted his gaze to Ro and held her in it.

She couldn't move. Couldn't blink. Couldn't take her eyes off of him. Cooper started whooping and holding his arms up in the air as if they were at an actual rock concert. When Winston got to the line about the lost hope that one day they'd be more than friends, Ro blushed furiously.

He broke his attention away from her, turning it towards the rest of his audience. As the song's intensity grew, so did Winston's execution. Cooper, Tomi and, especially, Tara, were impressed, enrapt. Watching wide-eyed as he carried them through the ballad like a professional. If Ro didn't know better, she would have sworn a spotlight had turned on and was shining only on Winston.

Ro was blown away. More than simply impressed, she was physically reacting to him. Her skin tingled whenever he turned his attention to her, which was often. As he clutched the microphone and let his body move with the rhythm of the music, her attraction to him was undeniable. Deep in her chest, her heart was fluttering.

When the song finished Cooper gave Winston a standing ovation, gesturing to the rest of them that they should stand up and cheer as well. Ro did. Her cheeks still hot. Her skin still tingling.

"Damn, brother, you can sing!" Cooper exclaimed, stepping to Winston's side and throwing his arm over his shoulders.

It was Winston's turn to blush. When he looked to Ro, his eyes were glittering, still caught up in the moment, still full of intense expression. He held her gaze once again. She tried to smile, but suddenly, without warning, Ro felt the urge to cry. She ducked her head and wiped the wisp of tears from her eyes with the back of her hand.

A horn blast interrupted their revelry. This was the signal that they were returning to dock. The trip was almost over. Cooper asked Winston if he would come with him to the helm and Ro watched the two of them leave. Cooper still laughing and jostling Winston around in congratulations for killing it at karaoke.

Ro watched them go, hugging herself as if she was cold, which she wasn't. Tara and Tomi flanked her, like two life sized, slightly tipsy Barbie dolls. They also watched the men go.

Tara spoke up, looking wryly at Ro as she said, "Single." She scoffed, "I don't think so."

Ro looked at her with confusion, "What?"

Tara nodded towards the door where the guys had just exited, "That boy's got it bad for you."

Ro's heart sped up, "Who?"

Tomi and Tara shared a look before Tomi chimed in, "If you don't know who, sweetie, you must be blind."

Chapter Twelve

As usual, Cooper did not show up in the office the next day. He was probably cruising on his new yacht with the bombshell twins, Ro knew. Two days ago she would have been jealous at that thought. Today, however, she wasn't so sure.

Late morning, she was called into a meeting with Alicia. Gloria attended in all of her quiet grace, efficiently tapping notes into her slender laptop while Alicia covered her agenda. They sat in Alicia's office, which was not as grand as Cooper's, but close. Her space was sleeker with less pomp and circumstance.

This was the first time Ro had met with Alicia in her office. The older woman and general manager of the Hotel Diamante was not apt to suffer fools, Ro knew this much about her from what little time they'd spent together. That's why Ro should have been on her best behavior. She should have tried to remain alert and appear competent. Having worked here for only one week, now was not the time to fall apart.

And yet there she was, slumping in her chair, fighting the

urge to yawn so often and so hard that her eyes watered madly. Ro looked rumpled today, not having had the time or energy to put into her appearance after getting home so late last night from the yacht trip. Though her eyes were watering like crazy, every time she blinked her eyelids scratched them like the backs of her eyelids were made of sandpaper.

"Miss Murray, are you listening?" Alicia's voice, balancing precariously between frosty formality and annoyance, cut through Ro's foggy brain.

"Yes, I'm sorry," she answered. She wasn't. Listening, that is. She was sorry. Ro was sorry that she seemed to be having a difficult time focusing on anything after last night. After spending all of that time with Cooper. After Winston sang.

"Would you like more coffee?" Gloria asked, pausing typing and furrowing her brow slightly at Ro.

"No, thank you," Ro said, stifling another yawn.

"You had a long day yesterday," Alicia stated. Not accusatory exactly, but definitely with a note of displeasure.

"Yes, again, I'm sorry," Ro perked up a little. How did Alicia know about the yacht trip?

Alicia looked sharply over the top of her black-rimmed glasses at Ro, then shifted her eyes to Gloria. Gloria seemed to understand what her boss wanted almost immediately. She turned in her chair so she was facing Ro more squarely, then placed a cool, dry hand on Ro's knee.

"Little one," Gloria said with kindness in her eyes. "We are..." she looked for the right word, glancing to Alicia and back to Ro before continuing, "We are concerned that your emotions are overwhelming you."

Now Ro was completely awake. Fear and humiliation rushed through her system, overcoming her fatigue. Was she getting fired? How much did these two women know about her man crush issues?

"Wha-?" Her voice croaked like a frog. Ro cleared her

throat and started again, "What do you mean?" She straightened her back in an attempt to look as prim and in control as they did.

"Did you spend yesterday afternoon and evening with Mr. Rivera...away from the office?" Alicia asked.

Ro stiffened. Not sure if this was the hammer coming down about inappropriate behavior or if they assumed she hadn't been getting her work done.

"Yes, he asked me to come to the dock and join him," she answered carefully. She didn't want to sound like she was dodging blame for anything, but technically he was her boss, wasn't he? "I'm not behind on work or anything like that," she added.

"No, that's not what's troubling us," Gloria reassured.

Alicia let out a short sigh, like someone who has been through a trying ordeal a hundred times and is about to go through it again. Her shoulders relaxed and some of her professional demeanor slipped away. She took off her glasses and placed them on her desk, leaning forward as she did. Ro could see a small sliver of what it must be like to be friends with Alicia, instead of an employee at her hotel.

"With all due respect to Mr. Rivera, we want you to understand that he is a man who enjoys the company of women," Alicia's face softened. "Many, many women," she added, tilting her chin down and raising her eyebrows to try and make her meaning more clear.

"Oh," Ro said. Her fear of being fired dissipated, but it was instantly replaced with embarrassment. As if she had been the unwitting participant in a prank. The butt of a joke.

Gloria patted her knee again, giving her a kind smile.

"I am assuming your outing with Mr. Rivera went into the evening?" Alicia asked, leaning back and picking up her glasses. Back to business.

"Um, yes, we didn't get back until late," Ro answered. She

felt the urge to explain that she hadn't been alone with Cooper. Nothing had happened. But the words didn't come out.

"Then you will take this afternoon off," Alicia said, "I think you may need the rest?"

Ro nodded mutely.

❧

A RHYTHMIC WHIRRING FILLED her ears as the ceiling fan spun and sent a steady flow of barely cool air across her face, her chest, arms and legs. The only other sound in her room was the occasional filtered squeal or shout coming from guests, probably children or teenagers, playing in the hotel pool outside her balcony. None of those sounds penetrated her focus on the turning blades of the ceiling fan. Ro's mind was far away.

After the meeting, she'd come back to her room and crawled into bed. Thoughts and emotions were all jumbled up and pumping through her body so hard she couldn't single out any one of them, let alone sort them out. Eventually, Ro had fallen into a fitful sleep. For how long she did not know. When she woke it was to the whirring of the ceiling fan and nothing else. Face up on the bed and still fully dressed, she was alone. Deeply alone.

Two hot, fat tears welled up in her eyes so quickly that they spilled out almost immediately, leaving streaks of wetness on her skin before pooling at her ears. More followed. Ro didn't move. She let the tears come, feeling them slide almost continually down the small patch of skin between her eyes and her temples, wetting her ears and hair. Time wasn't registering with her, but she stayed like that until her nose was too stuffed up to breathe.

Ro sighed and sat up. Only then noticing that she held

her cell phone in one hand. The black screen looked dead. A lump of technology, grey and unappealing, ready to be brought to life by a quick swipe of her thumb. She moved to do just that, compelled to...to what? Check her emails? Get on Instagram? Find Theo's profile and start scanning through his perfect life again?

She dropped the phone onto the bed in disgust and stood up, stalking into the bathroom. Ro flipped on the bathroom light and stood in front of the mirror. Her hair was sticking out in all directions, damp at her temples. Her eyes were puffy and red from crying. She looked hung over. Snatching some tissues from the box on the vanity, Ro blew her nose and wiped her eyes, then paused. She leaned forward and stared into her reflection.

"What are you doing?" She asked out loud, her voice throaty and cracking. The puffy eyed, red nosed version of herself stared back. Eyebrows pinched together and mouth screwed up in an attempt to control the crying. She didn't look like someone who was starting a new, adventurous life in an exotic place. She looked like the same old, heartbroken mess she'd been back in Indiana. Maybe she should take a picture of her reflection right now and post it on Instagram. Ro barked out a humorless laugh at the thought.

A light knock on the door of her room sounded. She hesitated before answering, maybe they would go away. The knocking sounded again.

Ro sighed and called out, "Hang on." She turned on the cold water and splashed her face with it, drying it on a thick, soft hand towel as she walked to the door. She peered through the peephole and saw that it was Carlos. When she opened the door to him, she saw that he had a rolling cart stacked with several covered dishes.

"Buenas tardes," Carlos said politely as he pushed the cart in through her door. If he was surprised at her appearance, he didn't show it. One side or Ro's mouth lifted in a half-smile. Carlos was a good sort of man. "Señora Alicia says I bring you food, because you do not eat," he explained as he parked the cart near her balcony doors. He turned and looked at her with his smiling, dark eyes. His brows furrowed slightly, "Is everything okay for you?"

"I'm fine, thank you, Carlos," Ro assuaged his concern. When his expression didn't lighten, Ro managed a smile and said, "I'm just a little tired."

This didn't do much to change his mind, but the promise to join him and his family for their early morning walk on the beach the next morning helped. He had a point. Ro needed to get out and explore the beauty of this place more. That was, after all, one of the reasons she had moved all this way.

Carlos excused himself from her room with gallant flourish, insisting that she call him if she needed anything at all. She swore she would and closed the door after him.

Delicious smells of onion and Chiles rose from the cart, making Ro's stomach rumble. Lifting the covers revealed ceviche, shrimp tacos, pico de gallo, and fresh corn tortillas, hot and steaming. She moved the dishes to her small table and looked into the pitcher to find an ice cold, bright red drink made with hibiscus. Very sweet and satisfying. Thankful for the spread, Ro poured a glass for herself and sat down to eat.

Munching on her first bite of ceviche, Ro savored the taste as she squinted out the window into the bright afternoon. A surge of thankfulness came over her. She still had her job and this beautiful place to live, not to mention all of the perks of working at a luxury boutique hotel. All of this obsessing over Cooper ended right now. Her urge to get involved with him was taking over her original goal, which was to have a wild and adventurous life. Winston had been right. She had a tendency to latch onto the kind of men that took her for granted. That, too, needed to be part of her New Year's resolution. She was not going to settle for a boring life or a sub-par relationship. Period.

Winston. Her stomach clenched at the thought of him. What was she going to do about Winston? Before she could spend another moment pondering that question, another knock sounded on her door.

Ro shook her head with amusement. Carlos was so funny. His attentiveness was over the top. She should take her cues from him when looking for her next relationship. If she could find a man who worried about her every need the way Carlos did, she would be a lucky woman.

"Coming," she called out as she hopped up and hurried to the door. "I swear, everything is del–" Ro started to say as she swung the door wide open.

She stopped short when she saw who was on the other side.

Chapter Thirteen

"Hey," Winston said, giving her a small wave from his hip.

An electric shiver ran up her arms and shoulders, as if he had somehow charged up the air on the other side of the door then blew it into her when she swung the door open. The sensation took her aback.

He wore swimming trunks and a T-shirt that read 'I heart Riviera Maya' on the front. The heart wasn't spelled out, but a big, fat, red cartoon heart. Just like the 'I heart New York' T-shirts. His sunglasses were folded and hung from the neck of the T-shirt. His brown hair, lightened by days spent in the sun and sea, was thicker and wavier than Ro had ever seen it. Tall, tanned and fit, he looked relaxed and confident, and sexy. To Ro's surprise, her stomach did a flip-flop.

"Carlos said you were off for the afternoon," he said. "I thought maybe you'd want to go swimming...with me," his voice broke a little at the pause.

Ro suddenly remembered how horrible she looked, and ducked her head as she half turned away from him.

"I was eating..." her voice trailed off.

Winston looked past her into her room, then back at her, "Smells good. I can wait for you, if you want to go." He smiled at her with a twinkle in his eyes, "There's a cenote about 20 minutes away from here that everyone says is really cool."

Ro had read about cenotes when she researched moving to Playa del Carmen. Of course, she had yet to explore one of them. She couldn't think of a snappy come back or a reason she shouldn't go with him. Actually, she kind of wanted to go with him.

"Sure," she shrugged and opened the door, stepping back so Winston could come in. As he walked by, the scent of him overwhelmed her senses. He smelled like sunshine and salt-water, like the beach with a little bit of coconut sunscreen mixed in. He smelled good.

"Good, you need to get out and experience some paradise!" Winston announced.

Her earlier feelings of gloom and doom weakened.

Soon she had finished her late lunch, sharing both the food and the delicious hibiscus drink with Winston. Then she changed into a yellow bikini and matching sarong she'd bought brand new before she moved here, but had yet had the chance to wear.

When she walked out of the bathroom in her new ensemble, Winston's hand froze at his mouth where he'd been about to take a swig of his drink. He swallowed hard and Ro felt a surge of that same crackling electricity.

"You look beautiful," he said.

Ro tried not to blush, but she wasn't sure it worked. She put her sunglasses on to avoid looking at him.

Winston insisted she slather on sunscreen. She couldn't reach her back, so he helped. His fingers were warm and firm as they made circles across her shoulders and down her spine.

His body so close behind hers, his fingers on her naked skin, the deep tones of his voice speaking so close to her neck as he talked about the cenotes in the area, all of this woke a hundred butterflies in her stomach.

When she was sufficiently covered in sunscreen they left. He took her downstairs and out the back entrance of the hotel into the alley where a small, beater of a car was parked haphazardly next to some trash cans.

"You're driving?" She hesitated, eyeing the two-door rust bucket Winston was unlocking.

"Yeah," he opened the passenger door for her and made a gallant sweeping motion with his arm to indicate she should enter.

"Where did you get this horrible form of transportation?" Ro asked with a laugh as she climbed in.

"It's Zander's. He leant it to me," Winston closed her door carefully and got into the driver's seat. When he started the engine it sputtered and belched out a plume of exhaust. Ro was certain the engine was about to die, but it chugged for a few seconds then settled into a more consistent puttering sound.

Winston wiggled his eyebrows at her, pulling his sunglasses out from his T-shirt and putting them on as he said, "We're off on an adventure!"

Ro laughed, then squealed as he put the car in gear and raced it recklessly through the alley into the street.

Despite crowds of pedestrians darting in and out of the streets, and honking cars, trucks and taxi cabs that were not following most, if not all, of what Ro considered basic traffic rules, Winston navigated Zander's funny little car successfully through the more populated city area. Soon they were on a two-lane highway that headed out of town towards El Jardin Cenote. Their destination.

There was no air-conditioning in the little car, so they

kept their windows down. The warm, humid air pummeled them from all directions and made conversation impossible. To combat the noise of the wind, Winston turned the old radio up and blasted Mariachi music from a local station. Ro's hair whipped around her face. She stretched her arm out the window and let it ride the pressure wave of speed against the fresh, heavy air of the countryside.

They buzzed past huge, ropey trees with deep green plumage, broken down buildings that may have been snack shops or small grocery stores, but Ro couldn't read the Spanish on the signs to know for sure, and a gas station that looked like it had seen better days. A lone Mexican man, who looked like he must be at least 80-years old, pumped gas into an ancient light blue pickup truck. This was the only way Ro knew the gas station was still operational and hadn't been condemned. Further past these roadside landmarks there was only a sea of dark green trees that extended into the far distance.

She looked over at Winston, whose own hair was being tossed around by the current inside of the car. He looked back and grinned widely, giving her a thumbs up.

"You okay?" He shouted over the noise.

Ro nodded and gave her own thumbs up in return. As chaotic and rough as this excursion was compared to her other experiences in Playa del Carmen, she was enjoying it. This was probably closer to the real Playa del Carmen anyway. Being away from the protections of the hotel and the watchful eye of Alicia, Gloria and Carlos, not to mention the over the top luxury of Cooper's existence, made it all the more exciting.

At the highway sign for Barcelo Maya Beach Resort there was another hand painted sign on the opposite side of the road, It read 'CENOTES – El Jardin del Eden – The Best – El

Mejor'. Winston slowed the car and turned onto a sandy road lined with fat palm trees that led them into the deep green of the surrounding jungle. Another hand made sign, on this one the message, 'Welcome, Eden Cenote' was burned into the wood instead of painted. The sign leaned against a stone wall where an open iron gate ushered them further down the bumping sandy road.

When they finally reached the cenote, Winston shelled out 200 pesos for each of them. They picked out snorkeling gear and a bottle of flavored water offered by the friendly attendant. Then they made their way along one of many pathways that led to the edge of the cenote.

Cenotes, Ro had discovered in her research, were naturally formed sinkholes that occurred when the limestone collapsed ages ago. These large openings exposed groundwater and became open to entrance from the top. They were especially found here, in the Yucatán peninsula and renowned as places to snorkel and scuba dive worldwide. She had always thought of them as something like a pond or a large, deep swimming pool. Standing directly next to one, Ro realized that they were much, much more than that.

"Wow," Winston said. He leaned forward and peered over the rocky edge and the sharp drop towards the water, "This is pretty cool."

"It is, isn't it?"

A thrill shimmied down her spine. They had seen a huge cenote at the Mayan ruins, the water level more than 30 feet down. So deep that anyone falling in would not be able to get out without assistance from the top. Paco had told them that the cenote was probably used for human sacrifice, which was chilling.

This one, however, was much more inviting. It had what looked like a cliff side, maybe 15 feet tall, where you could jump into the deep water below. But it also had stairs that had been built to take you from the top to the surface of the water, as well as several areas along the edges where the stones were easier to navigate. There was not beach to walk serenely to the water's edge, but you could climb easily enough in, and out again, from many points along the edge.

Surrounded by the jungle with sandy ground underneath, the park was punctuated by areas with picnic tables and benches so you could rest between swimming. Large rocks protruded up through the water of the cenote, offering places for swimmers to sit and rest while still sitting waist deep in the cool water or just out of its reach.

"Ready?" Winston asked as he pulled his T-shirt over his head, revealing his tan, muscled chest. Ro was temporarily distracted from their surroundings by this view, but pulled herself together and nodded with enthusiasm.

They spent the next hour swimming and snorkeling through all of the nooks and crannies of this beautiful place. Tiny, colorful fish surrounded them then swam away. Lazy iguanas watched them from the shoreline where they warmed themselves in the sun. Throughout the adventure, Winston would often turn to her and offer his hand to pull her towards a particularly interesting place, or swim so close to her while they were snorkeling that their arms or legs would gently tangle and untangle as they moved through the water.

Ro found these moments tantalizing. Being underwater with Winston was delicious, their bodies softly skimming one another's warm skin in the cool water. She wondered what it would feel like if he slipped his hand purposefully around her waist, or up her exposed stomach and along her ribs toward her bikini top.

She found that her own hands wandered naturally and freely in his direction, often coming into contact with his well formed biceps, or the muscles of his back and shoulders. She noticed how his abdomen flexed and moved as he swam and wondered what it would be like to run her finger along those muscles. She didn't do it, of course. But she couldn't stop herself from thinking about it.

"Want to take a break?" Winston asked.

"Sure."

They swam to one of the flat rocks that lifted out of the water in the center of the swimming area. Abandoned by a group of teens who had been sunning themselves on it earlier, it was the perfect size for Winston and Ro to stretch out on their backs next to each other and rest.

The sunshine felt good after being in the cool water for so long. And the exertion of swimming had tired her out in the most relaxing of ways. All of the worry and emotion she'd felt earlier in the day had simply been washed away by this beautiful cenote. Ro let out a contented sigh.

"I could get used to this," she said.

Winston chuckled, a pleasing, deep rumble from his chest, "You can get used to it. You live here, now, remember?"

"Oh, that's right," she answered with delight, as if she'd just realized this fact.

"There are tons of cenotes all around this area. Each one has its own, unique characteristics. Some of them are more underground and you're swimming in a huge cave," Winston explained with obvious interest. "You could map them out and go to each one if you wanted," he added.

Ro considered this for a moment, then answered, "Maybe I will. That sounds fun!"

"It would be fun," he answered. There was a wistful note in his tone and Ro turned her head to look at him. Tiny beads of water still clung to his skin. Because it was wet, his hair looked almost black, and it stuck out in all directions as it dried in the sun. She gazed at his profile. She'd never noticed how strong Winston's nose was, how his jaw was square and firm, how his lips were full. She'd only ever noticed how easily he smiled at her, and how much fun they had together.

"You seem to enjoy being on vacation," she said.

He turned his face to hers, it was only inches away. If she leaned in his direction, just barely, their lips might touch.

"I'm going home in two days," he said quietly.

"What? I thought you were staying for a month?" She was shocked at his news. More than that, she was disappointed.

"Nah," he turned back to face the sky, effectively avoiding eye contact, "I figure it's about time I go home."

His words sounded empty, not fully formed. Or not fully informative. Ro continued looking at him, her face twisting into a scowl. She didn't like being lied to, and she could tell that Winston was, at the very least, not telling her the whole truth.

Her gaze bored into him long enough that he turned back to her, exasperated, "What?"

"You know what. You're not telling me everything," she said.

He coughed out a laugh, "I'm not? What's my big secret?"

"I don't know, it's your secret," she answered. She meant for it to be friendly banter, joking between buddies, the light-hearted way they'd always been together. But the words came out softer than she intended, filled with sadness.

The jocular smile on Winston's face faded as he looked into her eyes. She wanted to say something more to him, make him tell her what he was thinking, explain why he was leaving, but there was a lump in her throat. Winston's jaw flexed. His deep, brown eyes traced her cheek and landed on her mouth where they lingered until Ro could feel blood rush into her lips, anticipating a kiss.

With no warning, Winston turned his face back to the sky with a frustrated sigh. He made fists with his hands and pressed them into his closed eyes, turning his head back and forth in an exaggerated 'no' motion.

"Okay, okay, okay," he said. He moved his arms back to his sides where they stayed, stiff and unmoving. "I can't believe this," he mumbled, more to himself than to Ro. He took in a deep breath and blew it out of pursed lips, calming himself. Then he cleared his throat and began, his face still aimed towards the sky, "I have something to tell you. Because, you know, I'm going back home and you're staying here and if I didn't tell you then I would always wonder what would have happened if I did." He turned back to her and Ro's heart started thumping in her chest. "You know I've never taken vacations," he paused, waiting for her to indicate she knew this was a fact.

"Right," Ro said quietly, nodding once.

"And you know that I always said it was because I loved my job so much. That I loved my career and my office and the work, everything."

Ro nodded again.

"The thing is, Ro, you have to believe me on this, I really thought that was true. All these years I thought I loved my job."

Ro furrowed her brow, "You don't?"

"No. The work is fine," Winston explained. He lifted his hand and flicked it in the air as if shooing away a fly, "That's not the point. That's not what I want to say."

Ro waited. He seemed to be building up to something and she didn't want to interrupt him.

"But then you left."

Ro's heart thudded even louder. A tingling dizziness flooded through her head and chest.

Winston sighed again and dipped his head so when he looked at her, he was looking up through his still damp locks of hair. Confessing a secret.

"You know why I never used my vacation time? Because you were there, at work. And I didn't want to miss a moment of time that I could be with you. When you left everything was empty. I was empty. That's when I figured it out. After all this time I finally figured it out. It's not the job I love...it's you."

Chapter Fourteen

Ro knew he was telling her the truth. As soon as the words left his mouth, she realized that she'd known Winston was in love with her for a long time. This fact had silently drifted in between them for years. She had grown used to it. Counted on it.

In the moments after he told her the space separating them seemed to solidify. Locked them in. Held them both captive to the other so that neither of them moved. Ro's heart seemed to beat out of her chest as she gazed into his beautiful, searching eyes.

The people playing in the water nearby, the sunshine of late afternoon, the shimmering water that lapped at the edge of their rock, all of this slipped away. What remained was a bubble that surrounded them, protected them from the outside world.

For a moment.

That moment was full of truth and love and possibilities. But the soaring feeling Ro had first felt upon hearing Winston's words soon faltered, stalled out and started to drop. And though truth and love remained floating around them, the feeling of possibility waned.

She watched him realize this. Observed quietly, meekly, as the expected response never came from her lips and the look in his eyes shifted from love and adoration to pain. There were no words that would ease this pain. So she said nothing. After what felt like forever and no time at all, Winston, her best friend, her confidante, withdrew his heart from the table.

Without saying a thing he turned away and sat up on the edge of the rock. Using his hands to support his weight, he lowered his body off the edge and sank into the water, pushing off and swimming away from her.

A piece of her heart tore off and left with him. Still she could not speak. Could not call him back. She didn't know why, but the words wouldn't come. All that came were hot, silent tears.

Riding back to town in Zander's crappy little car, the windows down, the wind whipping around them once more, there was a void between them. A chasm. Winston was silent, stony. Ro took every nuance of his mood as a punch in the stomach. She didn't want to be the cause of his pain, but she couldn't return his confession of love.

When he pulled up in the street in front of the hotel she mustered enough courage to ask, "Do you want to grab dinner?"

He shook his head and mumbled, "I've got to get Zander's car back. Not very hungry, anyway."

Ro nodded. There was a heaviness in the pit of her stomach, like she had swallowed some of the smooth stones along the edge of the cenote. She stepped out of the car onto the sidewalk in front of the hotel. Before closing the door, Ro bent down to say goodbye. When Winston gave her a begrudging glance his eyes were dark and distant. She couldn't form any words. She tried to smile, but even that seemed wrong. Crooked and awkward.

Winston looked down at his hands holding the steering wheel. An impatient taxi behind them honked their horn. Winston turned his head and glanced back at the taxi, then at Ro. His face softened slightly.

"I better get this thing moving," he said.

"Yeah," she felt tears pressing at the back of her throat and eyes. "Thank you for today," she managed.

He pressed his lips together and nodded, "Yeah, anytime. Bye, Ro."

"Bye," she said.

She shut the car door and Winston pulled away. The stones in her stomach started rolling and crunching together and Ro thought she might throw up.

That night she went to bed early, skipping dinner. She couldn't eat with the heavy weight in her stomach, and in her heart.

As she lay in her bed wishing sleep would come, memories of Winston played through her mind like movie clips. The way he always took her out for lunch on her birthday. That time he'd drawn her name for secret Santa and spent more than he was supposed to buying her the entire Harry Potter series in hardcover. She loved Harry Potter. All of the times he'd noticed when she got a new hairstyle or a new outfit. The laid back Friday afternoons they goofed off at work. The way he made her laugh in boring meetings, and over texts on the weekends, and just about any time she needed her mood lightened. The way he'd fussed over her when her engagement ended and she thought her heart was broken forever.

The memory that floated through her mind right before she fell asleep was of him today in the sunshine. Laying next to her on the rock in the middle of a cenote in the middle of the Yucatán Peninsula, where he'd come to make sure she was safe. She had never known anyone to care for her any better than Winston. This was the last conscious thought that drifted across her mind before sleep finally came.

❧

THE NEXT MORNING Ro joined Carlos and his family for their routine sunrise walk along the beach. The brilliant pinks and oranges of the Caribbean sunrise filled the sky. The ocean was transitioning from its deep turquoise of night to the sparkling bright blue of day. Waves rolled rhythmically onto the sand. She normally found that sound relaxing. Today, however, Ro was wrapped in melancholy.

"Mira, Señorita, mira," Carlos' son and daughter called to her, showing off as they ran to the very edge of the water and waited for a wave, then raced as fast as their little legs would carry them to escape the water.

Ro smiled at them. But her smile faded as soon as they looked away, inviting Carlos' special brand of concern.

"All is good for you, Señorita?" His face was full of worry.

"Yes, yes, thank you...gracias," Ro said, trying to give him a reassuring smile.

Josefina, quiet and sweet as always, hooked her arm in Ro's as they strolled. Ro was almost positive Josefina understood she was having man trouble. Women understood women, and some things crossed language barriers.

A shout of recognition reached them from a short distance away. They all turned in unison to see who was calling out. Two figures moved towards them. At the sight of them, Ro's heart jumped into her throat.

Winston and Cooper.

All politeness, Carlos paused and waited for the men to catch up. Ro had no choice but to wait as well. When they reached them, Cooper was all smiles.

"Good morning," Cooper said, his exuberance about whatever adventure he and Winston were starting off on was obvious.

"Señor Rivera, Señor Winston," Carlos ducked his head in a half-bow kind of greeting. Josefina smiled and blushed, averting her eyes under Cooper's toothy grin.

"Anyone up for some scuba diving today?" Cooper asked with enthusiasm. "That's where we're headed," he indicated Winston with a quick jerk of his head.

Winston didn't respond. He stood a little behind Cooper with his hands shoved into his pockets. He didn't even glance in Ro's direction.

Cooper, on the other hand, focused in on her and said, "Your boy is quite the diver for a newbie."

Her boy.

The phrase ignited heat in her cheeks and a sickening feeling in her stomach. Ro shook her head and said something unintelligible, all while trying to avoid looking at any of them, especially Winston.

She felt Josefina's grip tighten on her arm. She knew. Everyone knew. How could they not? Body language was easier to understand than the spoken word. And the body language between Ro and Winston right now was the most awkward, painful interaction imaginable.

Of course, Cooper was unaware. Either that, or he just chose to push his way through the awkwardness to get to what he wanted.

"Not today, gracias," Carlos said. As if he would ever give up his post at the hotel to go on a random scuba diving trip. Carlos was the most dedicated worker Ro had ever met.

"Maybe another time, then," Cooper said. She was sure he knew Carlos would never go, no matter how many times he was invited. Cooper zeroed in on her, "Ro?"

She looked up. She had to. She couldn't ignore her boss.

And even if he wasn't her boss he wasn't the type of man that got ignored.

"You coming with us?" Cooper asked.

Ro flicked her eyes between Cooper and Winston, every time they landed on Winston she felt a stab of anguish in her heart. She shook her head 'no'.

"I'm helping Gloria today," she said. It wasn't a total lie. Most days she did help Gloria.

Cooper shrugged and they said their goodbyes. Cooper with gusto. Winston more quietly. She let her gaze follow them as they made their way towards Zander's dive shop. Melancholy wrapped more firmly around her, like a boa constrictor. Winston would never be, as Cooper had put it, 'her boy'.

At work the same dull sadness persisted, following her around like a little grey cloud. After she completed her meager tasks at her desk, she moved to Gloria's office to help her with some data entry and bill paying. While they worked Gloria tried to engage Ro in conversation. And Ro attempted to be perky.

"We missed you at dinner last night," Gloria said.

"I went straight to bed when I got back. I was really tired," Ro responded.

"Oh? What made you so tired?"

"We went to El Jardin Cenote to swim."

"Oh, how nice," Gloria smiled. Then asked, "Who did you go with?"

Ro had to swallow to keep up her perky voice, "Winston."

"Mmm," was all the older woman said. After a few moments she added, "He's a nice young man, isn't he?"

Ro nodded and managed a bright, chirpy, "Yes."

Gloria gave a small grunt of approval and continued working. But Ro struggled to focus. Her mind continually drifted to Winston and fogged up her concentration.

"Is he moving here like you?" Gloria asked, keeping her eyes on her computer screen.

"No. He's leaving," her cheery facade almost cracked. But she managed to explain, "He has to go back to work."

"I see," Gloria sounded a little let down. They worked silently for a few minutes until Gloria spoke again, "I was married for 37 years to my wonderful Fernando." She looked at Ro with soft eyes when she said his name. So sweet. "He had a good job at his father's ranch when we met. And he fell in love with me right away. He always said he was crazy in love with me before I even knew his name," Gloria chuckled quietly at this memory.

Ro listened with interest. A good love story might cheer her up.

"But I was young and full of adventure, and I didn't want to live in the country. I thought it was boring. I wanted to do other things besides have a husband and children," Gloria continued.

"You did?"

Gloria nodded emphatically, "Oh, this was a very unpopular view for a young lady to take, especially back then."

"I bet."

"But Fernando loved me with passion anyway. I left my family and moved to Playa del Carmen and started working as a maid in this hotel," Gloria tapped a pointed finger on the surface of her desk.

"Really?" Ro was impressed. Though she couldn't say she was totally surprised. Gloria may be small, but her strength was palpable.

Gloria nodded, her eyes glowing with happiness at the memory, "And do you know what my Fernando did?"

"What?"

"He followed me," Gloria leaned toward Ro and placed her hand on the young woman's knee, patting it warmly. "He told his father to give his place at the ranch to his younger brother because he was not returning, and he followed me here. He got a job at a construction company and we were married," she turned back to her work, giving Ro another meaningful look as she did.

Ro loved this story, and she was sure Gloria was telling her for a reason. Anyone with as keen an eye as Gloria's could tell something was going on between her and Winston. But the older woman refrained from looking at her again, leaving her to her thoughts. Ro was thankful for that, because her mind was whirling. A flurry of butterflies filled her stomach as well, as if revived by a cool, fresh breeze.

The door to Alicia's office opened and both Gloria and Ro looked up. Alicia, though calm, held the air of an emergency around her. She was holding her cell phone and her eyes were eagle-like behind her black-rimmed glasses.

"Mr. Rivera just called. There's been a diving accident and he's en route to the hospital."

Chapter Fifteen

Gloria immediately went into action, smoothly picking up the receiver of her slim lined desk phone and dialing a number. Any activity seemed impossible to Ro. Sitting stupidly in her chair, her face was frozen in shock. All she could do was ask short, stilted questions.

"Is Cooper okay?"

"He is fine, apparently it was someone on the boat with him," Alicia answered, her gaze moving swiftly to Ro then back to Gloria.

An invisible hand gripped Ro's heart. If Cooper was all right, then who was injured?

Outside, the cabbie who had taken them to the dress shop sped up to the curb and parked in front of them. The old gentleman hurried out of the driver's seat and ushered Ro and Gloria into the back of the cab.

"Where's the hospital?" Ro asked dumbly. Her tongue was almost numb. She gripped her hands tightly in her lap to try and keep them from trembling.

"It's close," Gloria said.

Just she and Ro would go to the hospital. Since the injured

party was not Cooper, Alicia remained behind to await updates from Gloria.

The ride felt like an eternity. The fingers that had slipped around Ro's heart earlier turned icy cold and squeezed. If Cooper wasn't hurt, it was possible that Winston was the one being rushed to the hospital. She could text or call him to find out, but something deep inside of her was too terrified. What if he didn't respond?

Every time a thought of him being pulled out of the water, or carried on a stretcher, or in a hospital bed with tubes and machines hooked up to him, entered her mind, the icy fingers gripped her heart even tighter and she couldn't breathe. She had to put any thoughts out of her mind and concentrate on breathing. In through her nose, out through her mouth.

When they arrived and walked through the front doors of the modest two-story hospital building, Gloria began speaking to a young woman at the receptionist desk in rapid fire Spanish. Ro couldn't understand a word of it. She waited behind the older woman as information was exchanged, breathing in through her nose and out through her mouth. A man in scrubs approached and led them into the hospital.

Not only were the conversations around her in Spanish, it seemed to Ro that the voices were echoing, getting deeper and slower. Their footsteps were muffled, like from a dream. For a hallway in a hospital, the space seemed dark and narrow. Ro blinked hard and the darkness receded. Tunnel vision. Her knees felt wobbly.

Just ahead Ro saw a man stand up from a dark blue plastic chair that was set outside a hospital room. It was Cooper. There was nobody with him.

Ro tried to speak, but her lips wouldn't move. Winston wasn't waiting in the hallway. He must be in the hospital room. She watched Cooper's expression change from the relief of seeing them to panic as his gaze moved past Gloria to her. He lunged forward just as the blackness filled her vision.

A strong hand held her around the waist. She was leaning on something warm, very warm. A body. A person. A chest. She sucked in a breath and smelled sunshine and sea salt and coconut sunscreen.

"You all right?" The voice rumbled into her ear. A familiar voice. Winston's voice.

Her vision began to clear. Her cheek was pressed firmly into a man's chest. She turned her eyes up and into Winston's face, so close to hers, full of concern.

Winston had one arm around her waist and was holding her firmly to his body, leaning his torso away from her slightly in order to support her shoulders and head. In his other hand he was holding a steaming cup of coffee.

Cooper stood in front of them. He'd lunged forward in order to catch her as she fainted. But Winston had been faster.

"Here's your coffee," Winston handed the cup to Cooper.

"Thanks," Cooper said. He was eyeing Ro warily, "Are you okay?"

Embarrassed, relieved, her head still spinning, Ro tried to nod 'yes'. Winston took hold of her upper arm with his newly freed hand. Suddenly, Ro was overcome with emotion and she pressed her face into his chest, letting him wrap his arms around her completely as she wept quietly.

"Hey, hey," Winston said softly into her hair.

"I'm sorry," she sniffled into his T-shirt.

"Everything's okay. Here, let's get you a chair," Winston said.

She shook her head defiantly and stayed pressed into him, his strong arms surrounding her. She didn't want to sit down, she only wanted him to hold her and know that he was safe. That she was safe with him.

She did sit, after all. There were two plastic chairs and as soon as she'd calmed down Winston made sure she sat in one of them. Gloria had the other one. Winston left to get them both something to drink from the vending machine where he'd found the coffee. Ro was wiping the wetness from her eyes with the backs of her hands as he left, watching him.

Just before he disappeared around a corner, Winston turned and walked backwards so he could look at her. She met his gaze and smiled through her drying tears. His face lit up into an ear-to-ear grin that was so bright it melted the cold fingers of dread that had held her heart on the way to the hospital, leaving her warm and tingly all over.

"Who is the injured diver?" Gloria was asking.

Ro felt like a real jerk. Overcome by relief that Winston was okay, she'd forgotten all about whoever was in with the doctor.

"Zander, but he's fine," Cooper answered.

Gloria sniffed, "Not too fine if he is here."

"What happened to him?" Ro asked.

"He got stung on the elbow by a Scorpion fish. He was trying to make an adjustment on his camera and jabbed his elbow back into the thing," Cooper explained.

"He'll be okay?" Ro asked.

"Oh, yeah. He definitely needs to be treated. They're poisonous. But now that he's here, I'm sure he'll be fine."

Cooper sipped his coffee. He'd obviously been in the ocean water and looked even more handsome because of it. He wore his normal style, James Bond crossed with yacht club chic. It looked good on him, as everything always did. He had been watching Ro carefully and out of nowhere crouched down in front of her, putting his free hand on her knee. The movement surprised her and she leaned back a little.

"Are you sure you're okay?" Cooper asked. His eyebrows were knit together and he rubbed small circles on her knee with his thumb, the motion making his hand edge further up on her thigh.

"Oh, I'm fine. I just got a little woozy in the car and...and I always feel a little weird in hospitals."

"Me, too!" Cooper said.

When he spoke he shifted his weight slightly and used Ro's leg to steady himself. This moved his hand even further up her leg. It was in the middle of her thigh now, his fingertips under her skirt, his forearm rested against her knee.

Ro became very aware of Cooper's physical presence. His sea tossed hair had dried in that way that only happens on the beach. This close up, the width of his shoulders almost made her claustrophobic. The muscles of his arm flexed. His fingertips grazed her bare thigh, tickling her skin. She couldn't tell if he was making a move on her or had gotten too close by accident, out of concern.

"Well, we'll be out of here soon. And hopefully not be back!" He said, laughing.

Ro nodded and laughed with him as he leaned forward to get in a position where he could straighten up. As he leaned in, his mouth came very close to her cheek. Close enough he could have kissed her if he'd been inclined. Flustered by this thought, Ro giggled. Just as Cooper stood, she glanced down the hallway and saw Winston halted abruptly, holding two steaming cups of coffee. Confusion filled his eyes.

From that distance he could easily have assumed that Cooper had just kissed her. And that she had responded with a flirtatious giggle. Ro made a move to stand. She wanted to go to Winston, to make sure he understood that wasn't what had happened. Before she could, the door to the hospital room opened and the doctor and two nurses stepped out.

From that point on there was a flurry of activity surrounding Zander, who lay irritated and restless in the hospital bed. Between Cooper taking over and asking questions in English while Gloria tried to interpret, and Zander declaring his fitness to be released from the hospital, then enduring bouts of pain bad enough they made him curse, the whole situation was rather chaotic. Winston silently delivered the coffee to her and Gloria, avoiding eye contact as he did.

She wished he would look at her. She wanted to somehow reassure him that she hadn't been flirting with Cooper. But he was busy offering Zander help and friendship, and she couldn't very well interrupt just to appease her own feelings. Zander was the one in trouble here, not her. After making such a scene with her fainting spell, she refused to follow Winston around like a needy, insecure girlfriend. She would wait until they were back at the hotel, alone.

That, it turned out, wasn't going to happen for a while.

It was decided that Gloria and Ro were no longer needed at the hospital. Nor was Cooper. Winston volunteered to stay with Zander and escort him home safely when he was released. Cooper was relieved to be released of the responsibility, which bothered Ro. Zander had been Cooper's friend longer than Winston's. Now that they all knew Zander was going to be fine, Cooper was bored with this scene and ready to get back to something more fun. They left Winston standing next to Zander's hospital bed and Ro was embarrassed for Cooper's lack of maturity.

She made sure to say to Winston as they left, "I'll see you back at the hotel?"

Winston nodded and gave her a small wave. Although he was looking at her, it felt like he was looking right through her.

Back at the office Cooper wanted to review his emails and actually give her some administrative tasks to do on his behalf. This was the first time he'd taken much of an interest in any real hotel business. Ro tried to concentrate, but found it difficult. Checking her phone discreetly every few minutes for any kind of message from Winston. None came.

Winston was a no show at dinner as well. After sweeping the dining area for him, Ro went to Carlos at the front desk.

"Has Winston come in yet?" She asked.

Carlos made a tsk-tsk sound and shook his head, "No, Señorita. He is not come by here this night."

With nowhere else to sit and wait, Ro took a stool at the hotel bar. The same dark shining wood that graced the rest of the hotel made its mark here as a long bar and floor to ceiling shelves set against a floor to ceiling mirror. The top of the bar was made of white marble, with veins of black and silver running through it. Ro ran her hand over the smooth, cool surface and ordered a citrus wine spritzer.

Hotel guests filled the room. They sat at the small tables or leaned against the bar, talking and laughing and sipping elaborate frozen concoctions. Mostly couples. Mostly in love, or at least on their way.

She sighed and took a sip of her drink. Bitter fizz ran over her tongue.

"What's a nice girl like you doing in a place like this?"

Ro saw him in the mirror first. Standing behind her, dressed to kill in a tight fitting, French blue shirt, no tie.

Cooper. His dark eyes gleaming, his perfectly shaped mouth curled into a sexy smile.

Surprised to see him, her spritzer went down the wrong tube, making her cough and splutter into her cocktail napkin. When she recovered, thankful none of it had sprayed out of her nose, she returned Cooper's smile.

Sliding onto the school next to hers, he nodded at the

bartender to bring him his usual. Leaning into the space between her shoulder and her ear, his breath brushed her skin.

"How are you, stranger?" He asked.

His breath wreaked of booze. Ro glanced behind him into the crowd.

"Is Tomi with you?" She felt the need to remind him that he had a girlfriend.

"Pffft," Cooper blew a raspberry into the air, sending a fine spray of spittle onto Ro's shoulder. "She's not ready yet. Can you believe that? It takes her hours to get ready to go out, it's ridiculous," he slurred the last few words of his sentence just as the bartender placed a heavy crystal glass in front of him full of amber liquor.

"Are you two going out?" Ro tried to steer the conversation. She wasn't Tomi's biggest fan, but she also wasn't interested in talking nasty about her behind her back.

"Probably...gotta get out of this rat hole," Cooper took a swig of his drink then his eyes widened. "Did I say that out loud?" He asked in mock horror, dropping his forehead until it leaned on her shoulder and laughing.

Ro didn't know what to say. Cooper had never been this physical with her, nor showed her this kind of attention. He lifted his head, but kept his arm on the back of her bar stool, shifting so their bodies remained close.

Just a few days before she would have been thrilled at this new development. Sitting close together in the sensual light of a bar, alone, no Tomi, no Winston in sight. But now everything was different. Ro glanced uncomfortably around the people milling in the bar, hoping that Winston didn't show up while Cooper was all over her and sloppy drunk.

The truth of her situation rippled through her body making her shiver. She didn't want Cooper anymore, not at all. She didn't want him because she already had Winston.

And Winston was the best thing that had ever happened to her. The instant that thought solidified in her mind, Ro's heart soared.

How could she have missed it all of this time? How could she have left him hanging after her told her that he loved her?

Ro gave her head a quick shake, brushing off the guilt. Yes, she'd been confused and surprised. But now she wasn't, and the moment Winston walked back into this hotel, she would tell him. She couldn't wait to see the look on his face.

"You look extra beautiful tonight, Ro," Cooper dripped the words into her ear, making her feel slimy. He let out a fluid chuckle and started singing quietly, "Row, row, row your boat, gently down the stream." This sent him into another bout of the giggles and he dropped his head onto her shoulder again.

Just as Ro was wondering how she was going to get rid of this overly friendly version of her jet-setting boss, a miracle happened. Tomi walked into the bar.

"Tomi!" Ro shouted at her over the noise and waved happily. Cooper sat up straight and looked in the direction she was waving. Ro had never thought she would be so happy to see the bleached blonde, Botox injected, lipo-suctioned vision of Tomi as she was in that moment. She was saved from Cooper's drunken advances and full of the knowledge that she finally knew what she wanted. Who she wanted.

Hours later, her excitement was more subdued. After being saved from Cooper by Tomi, she had waited in the bar for over two hours. Winston never showed up there or anywhere else at the hotel. Nor did he respond to her text asking if everything was okay. It got too late for her to walk down to Zander's dive shop and see if she could find him. Too may drunken partygoers in the streets at this time of night. Plus she didn't know if they were at the dive shop. She didn't know where Zander lived. Left with little alternative,

Ro went to bed. She would find him first thing in the morning.

That night she dreamed.

Standing on the beach, looking at the sunrise. Fine, white sand soft and warm under her bare toes. Her pure white gown billowed, light and gauzy, in the ocean breeze and Ro realized that she was getting married. A beach wedding. So romantic.

Under a pink sky, the turquoise water glittered and Ro walked down the sandy aisle that led to a grand arch. The arch was decorated with pink and white flowers growing thick on vines. Two men waited for her. One was her groom. The other was a preacher.

Ro floated past faceless guests seated in white folding chairs and finally arrived at the arch. Her groom turned to her with a charming smile. It was Cooper in a gold tuxedo.

"Wait," she said, but it came out as a whisper and nobody seemed to hear her.

The preacher started speaking in a monotone voice, so low she couldn't understand what he was saying. Her arm wouldn't move and she looked down to see that Cooper had a tight grip on her. Shaking her head, she pulled on her arm. It didn't budge.

Ro looked up to plead with Cooper to let her go and she heard someone giggling. Turning around to see who was laughing, she was greeted with the vision of Tomi and Tara in neon pink bridesmaid dresses. They had their hands over their mouths to try and muffle their laughter.

"No," she said in her mind. But no sound came out of her mouth.

She whirled around towards the preacher. Surely she could refuse to marry Cooper? Nobody would force her, would they?

The preacher's mouth opened and closed as he spoke.

Still, none of the words made sense. Cooper's grip tightened on her arm and Ro began to struggle to get away.

She looked beyond the preacher at the beach that stretched for miles and the shining blue ocean. If only she could free herself from Cooper, she could run past the preacher and escape.

Ro blinked into the shimmering orange ball that was the sun sitting on the edge of the horizon. A silhouette appeared from the center of this bright light, standing where the waves kissed the beach.

Everything went into slow motion. The preacher's mumbling, her bridesmaid's from hell giggling, even her arm trying to twist free from Cooper. The silhouette moved closer and closer to her as she watched. As she hoped.

Then, miraculously, her arm was free. She stumbled past the preacher, away from Cooper and towards the silhouette. It was a man's silhouette. It was Winston. Coming to save her.

She ran.

She could see Winston clearly now. He opened his arms wide. A smile full of joy on his face.

"Winston!" She cried out and her voice was no longer stuck in her throat.

Ro woke with a start. She had slept so fitfully that most of her covers had slipped onto the floor and her arm had become wrapped up in her sheet. Still, she was exuberant as she practically leapt out of bed.

Glancing at her window she could see the early glow of sunrise. This was a new day. She would find Winston today and they would start their life together.

Chapter Sixteen

Despite Ro's excitement to talk to Winston, she wanted to take a little time getting dressed. After all, if she was going to declare her love for someone she may as well look good while she did it. Besides, it was still early in the morning and she had plenty of time before she had to be at work.

Running a bath in the soaker tub, she poured in some of the jasmine and orange bath salts. As the tub filled and the scent permeated her room, she went to the closet and pulled out the white cotton lace dress she'd bought just before flying here. It was mid-length, with a sweetheart neckline and adorable puffy sleeves. She had bought it on a whim, thinking it would be perfect to go out to lunch or shopping in Playa del Carmen. But she hadn't had the chance to wear it anywhere yet. It had seemed too romantic to wear to the office.

"Romantic is perfect for today," she said out loud.

Smiling as she laid the dress out on her bed, butterflies in her stomach, she checked out the window. The sky was turning its glorious pink, meaning the sun would be completely up soon. Ro hurried into the bathroom to sink into the warm scented water.

It was not yet 8 o'clock when she approached the front desk. In her flirty white lace dress, thin leather sandals and a dainty gold heart necklace with matching bracelet, Ro felt feminine and ready for romance. Carlos was already at the desk.

"No beach walk this morning?" Normally he arrived at the front desk at 8:00 am sharp.

"No, Señorita, not this day. Josefina takes children to see their abuela...grandmother," he responded.

She nodded in understanding. Glancing around the lobby as casually as she could, Ro tried to ignore the nervous ball of energy trembling in the center of her belly. Without looking at Carlos, she asked nonchalantly, "Have you seen Winston this morning?"

Carlos sucked in his breath, making Ro look at him with concern. His normally warm and friendly expression had fallen. Giving her sad eyes, he clucked his tongue and shook his head slowly.

"He not tell you?" Carlos asked.

"Tell me what?" Ro's stomach dropped at the shift in his demeanor.

"Señor Winston left this morning."

"Left the hotel?"

"To the airport," Carlos delivered this last bit of bad news with a heavy heart.

The romantic bubble she'd been in all morning burst, shattering all of her intentions into a hundred pieces. She didn't know what to do. She simply stood there staring at Carlos with wide eyes.

Carlos rummaged for something on an unseen shelf behind the counter. He pulled out an envelope and placed it on the counter. She recognized the Hotel Diamante stationary. Her name was written in the center of the envelope in Winston's handwriting. 'Ro' looked small and lonely in the center of the thick, gleaming paper.

"He say to give this to you," Carlos pushed the envelope towards her and shook his head sadly at what a shame the whole drama was.

Carlos knew this was not a love letter. So did Ro. She stared at it for a moment, not wanting to touch it because then she would have to open it and read Winston's last words to her. That was not something she wanted to do.

A family of tourists, Mom and Dad with four children, converged on the front desk and Carlos turned to help them. Ro reached up and slid the envelope off of the counter, surprised it didn't burn her fingers when she touched it.

Overcome with the need to get the pain over with as quickly as possible, like ripping off a Band-Aid, she sat down on the nearest Victorian loveseat. The envelope was light. Not much to be said, she guessed. She sighed and slid her finger into the top corner to tear the top open. Her hands trembled slightly as she pulled the neatly folded paper out and opened it.

Ro,

Sorry for the handwritten note drama. This was too much for a text, and I couldn't talk to you in person about it. I was afraid nothing would come out right. So, handwritten note it is.

I've gone home. I was able to get an early flight this morning and took it. I don't want to intrude on your new life any longer. I know you love me as a friend, but that fact doesn't make watching you fall in love with someone else any easier. It might even make it harder. I might be able to move on if you hated me.

Scratch that. I hope you don't. Hate me, that is. I don't hate you for not loving me the way I love you. You can't help how you feel. And you should know that being your friend has been one of the greatest experiences of my life. Thank you for that. You're the funniest, kindest, most beautiful person I've ever known. You're the best, Ro. Don't ever forget.

I've got to get to the airport now. Best of luck on all of your new adventures. I hope you find everything you've ever wanted.

Love Always,
Winston

The noise in the busy lobby hushed. All Ro could hear was her heart pounding, sending blood rushing through her head. She breathed in, listening to the air filling her lungs. Staring at the words on the paper without reading them, she saw a fat tear drop onto the top of the letter, smearing her name. Her throat tightened. What had she done?

Ro ran her thumb across Winston's signature. So familiar. She choked back a sob and tore her gaze away from it, looking up towards the ceiling then letting her eyes wander across all of the tourists and staff bustling here and there in the lobby.

Had she really only been here two weeks? It seemed like a lifetime ago that she'd first entered the hotel. Yet it had only been days. She'd been so excited, so sure that this was what she wanted. And now as she took in the weekday morning rush knowing she had a place here, could build a new life here, she didn't know if she wanted to stay. Did she really belong here? Did any of her big plans to move to Mexico and live in paradise mean anything if she lost the most important person in her world?

Without Winston in her life nothing else seemed to matter.

She groaned and looked at the letter again. Slumping against the wall, she read his words over and over.

"I'm such a fool," she whispered to nobody.

"You're not a fool," a voice answered.

Ro jumped at the sound. Blinking, she looked up into Gloria's gentle, round face.

"Oh, Gloria," Ro's expression crumpled as tears spilled down her face.

"Now, now," Gloria sat next to her and put her arm around Ro's shoulders. Ro dropped her face into her hands to try and hide her break down from the general public. "Carlos says you are having a problem with your young man?"

Ro nodded emphatically, emitting a small moan from behind her cupped hands.

Gloria tsk-tsked as she tried to discreetly console Ro's blubbering.

"Perhaps we should find him and you can speak with him about how you're feeling?" Gloria offered.

Ro let her hands fall into her lap, the letter now crumpled and tear stained. She shook her head morosely and tried to stem her crying long enough to explain.

"H-he-he is g-g-gone," she wailed, turning her face into Gloria's shoulder.

"Gone to the airport, yes?" Gloria asked.

"Mmhmm," Ro sniffled.

"Carlos said he left one hour ago. I think, perhaps, his plane is still here?"

Ro stopped crying. She sat up and looked at Gloria with instant understanding.

"Of course!" She exclaimed, "Why didn't I think of that? I'm so dense!"

Gloria chuckled and shook her head, answering, "Love does that to us."

Time was of the essence. Ro's mind was whirling with how to get to the airport, how to figure out what flight he was on, and how to get him off of the flight if he'd already boarded. Frantic energy took over and she stood up quickly.

"I need to get a cab," she said urgently, looking from left to right and back again as if a cab could be found somewhere in the lobby.

"Yes," Gloria stood up next to her and calmly gestured towards the grey haired, mustached cabbie who was ever present whenever Gloria was around.

"Your chauffeur!" Ro could have cried tears of joy if she had the time.

Gloria steered Ro and Carlos to the cab that waited outside, and climbed in after them. She and Carlos would go along for "assistance", she explained.

Grateful for their help and consistently solid presence of mind, Ro tried to remain calm. Her mind bounced between all of the possibilities; they find Winston and she confesses her love for him, or he has already boarded the plane and they have to get someone in authority to inform him of her love for him, or his plane has already left and she doesn't get a chance to tell him how she feels, and he goes back to his old life and realizes what a ridiculous emotional wreck she really is, then forgets about her.

That would be bad, but there was one worse possibility.

What if they did find him and she was able to confess her love only to find out that she was too late? What if he'd changed his mind?

She shook her head sharply, willing that thought away. She felt a little sick after considering this outcome. Or, perhaps she was getting carsick.

They were racing, more like careening, towards the airport. Ignoring traffic signals, signs, pedestrians, the rights of other motorists, and maybe even the laws of physics, Gloria's chauffeur was doing everything possible to get them there swiftly. When they were finally on the highway that was a straight shot to the airport, Ro was afraid to look at the speedometer to see how fast they were going. Sitting in the back seat left her feeling queasy, but hopeful they might make it in time.

When they reached the airport, the cab screeched to a halt at the curb. Carlos jumped out to intervene with airport security, which was ample, while the chauffeur helped Gloria and Ro out of the back seat. Gloria took Ro's elbow firmly and directed her inside.

Gloria had been on her cell phone almost the entire drive. The one sided conversations all in Spanish had gone over Ro's head. But now that they were in the airport she got the idea Gloria had been requesting important flight information, because the older woman steered Ro decisively through throngs of travelers and past all of the airline ticket counters.

Finally, she stopped. A middle aged, barrel chested man with a double chin wearing a dark blue suit and tie, stood at attention at what appeared to be an empty gateway leading into the bowels of the airport. Upon seeing Gloria, the man's face lit up and he greeted her in Spanish. A gold nameplate pinned to his suit jacket read, "Eduardo Durazo, Director de Seguridad".

Carlos, breathing hard from running to catch up, appeared behind them. He gave Ro an encouraging smile and a thumbs up. After a few short exchanges of information and a gallant bow from Señor Durazo, they were ushered through the abandoned entryway into a long concourse with digital signs showing airline names and flight numbers. Permanent signs, each showing a gate number, went on and on down the concourse, until they were so far away she couldn't read them.

"What gate number? Do we know?" Ro asked, overwhelmed at the sheer number of them stretching into the distance.

Gloria nodded, "They said gate number 65."

All three of them looked up. They were standing under

the first gate number in the concourse. Gate number 28. They looked at each other in dismay.

"What time did they say it was leaving?" Ro asked with a sinking feeling in her stomach.

Gloria's eyes saddened, "Five minutes."

"Cuanto?" Carlos asked.

"Cinco minutos," Gloria told him again.

Ro knew it was an impossible task. By the time they got to the gate there would be no time left to stop the plane. It would already be pulling away from the building. The hope she'd held onto in the cab slid off of her and fell into a puddle on the floor.

"You love Señor Winston?" Carlos asked her, passion in his voice.

Ro looked into his eyes, her heart already crumpling from disappointment. He knew the answer because he'd watched her and Winston together, and he was a romantic at heart. Carlos truly felt her pain in this moment.

Ro nodded, barely able to say it out loud, "Yes. I love him."

A huge smile spread across his face and his eyes danced as he grabbed her shoulders, "We run, Señorita. We run!"

Lifted by his encouragement, Ro felt a thrill surge through her.

Gloria's eyes lit up and she nodded enthusiastically, "Go, go, go!"

So they ran.

Ro's sandals slapped the smooth, shiny floor as she sprinted down the concourse. Her puffy lace sleeves and skirt fluttered madly in the breeze caused by her body's momentum. Carlos weaved through the crowd a few steps in front of her, leading the way towards Gate 65. The joy he was experiencing taking part in this dramatic lover's reunion was apparent in the way he shouted encouraging comments to her over his shoulder as they ran.

Ro ran as fast as she'd ever run in her life. Her legs flew under her skirt and she followed Carlos with single-minded focus. She had to get to Winston before he left Mexico. She had to tell him she loved him, that she was in love with him. Every minute that went by and he didn't know that fact was a tragedy.

By the time they reached Gate 65 they were both winded. Breathing hard and sweating in the humidity, Ro and Carlos broke through the last wall of people blocking their path. As they burst into the waiting area they were greeted by absolutely nobody.

"Oh, no!" Ro cried out.

No passengers milled around waiting to board. No airline employees perched behind the counter assigned to Gate 65. The digital sign was turned off and the door leading out to the airplane was shut tight.

They hurried to the giant windows. The airplane carrying Winston out of her life had already pulled away from the edge of the building and was turning to get in line for take off on the runway.

Placing her palm on the smoke tinted glass, she leaned her forehead against the back of her hand and watched helplessly. Still breathing hard, the glass began to fog up in front of her face. A strong hand rested lightly on her shoulder. Carlos, as dejected and upset as she was, shook his head in dismay as he patted her shoulder in condolence.

They watched in silence as the plane moved out of their view. Ro squeezed her eyes shut against the sight, and against the tears that threatened to come. Her throat tightened as she held down the frustration that wanted to burst out.

She'd pushed him away. Sent him back to Indiana and out of her life. Of course he wasn't dead and she could talk to him over the phone. Maybe everything would work out in the end. Maybe.

They made their way back up the concourse and ran into Gloria on her way to meet them. Upon seeing Ro and Carlos, who was almost as upset as Ro over the matter, Gloria gave them both a soft, sad hug. Winston had gone back to America and they had failed in their mission to stop him. The three of them trudged back through the concourse with the air of people who had just watched a romantic movie that ended catastrophically.

Cloaked in gloom, her eyes cast down to the floor just in front of her, Ro concentrated on taking one step at a time. She could do nothing more. If she tried to speak she was afraid she would cry.

The trip back to the main section of the airport where all of the gift shops and restaurants were located seemed much longer than when she and Carlos had been racing the clock. Of course they'd been running and filled with a powerful sense of hope.

Ro had no such feeling now.

There was only emptiness. Longing. A vague sense of loss every time they passed people reuniting with their loved ones or arriving in Mexico for a fun filled vacation. Ro scowled at the obvious honeymooners disembarking from their flight. The sickening displays of love were like barbs in her heart. Even Michael Bolton's "When a Man Loves a Woman" played loudly from a nearby airport bar. The irony was almost too much.

She sighed. She had to get a grip. She had to stop comparing her love life to the rest of the world and get on with her life. Besides, it wasn't even Michael Bolton singing. It didn't sound like him. It sounded edgier.

Ro paused mid-stride, tilting her head to listen more carefully. She turned her attention to the chalkboard sign outside of the bar. Scrawled in multi-colored chalk under the heading 'Cancún Beach Bar', written in all caps, was one word, KARAOKE.

The words of the song wrapped around her and pulled her towards the open door of the bar. Stepping into the airport version of Cancún, complete with fake thatch roofed bar and a mural of scuba divers exploring a vibrant coral reef, Ro saw him. He stood on a small stage set aside for live music. Belting out the chorus to the song with his eyes closed and the microphone held expertly to his mouth, was Winston.

"Señori–" Carlos began, stopping short just behind her as he caught sight of Winston singing.

Ro tried to say something, but her heart was in her throat. She tried to move, but her feet seemed glued to the floor. She tried to wrap her mind around what she was seeing and found herself feeling dizzy and unable to catch her breath. For the second time in as many days Ro thought she was about to faint.

"Go to him, hija," Gloria said, placing her hand on Ro's back. Carlos, bless him, took hold of her elbow to try and steady her. Emboldened by their encouragement, Ro took in a shuddering breath and stepped towards the stage.

It took Winston a few moments to notice her as she emerged out of several groups of tourists who were killing time in the bar. It took a few more moments for him to register what he was seeing. When he did, Winston froze. The accompaniment track kept playing, but he was no longer singing along. He had stopped on the 'please don't treat me bad' line and was staring at her.

All eyes turned to Ro. Her white lace dress glowing in the stage lights, her face turned up towards Winston. She responded to his surprise with a steady gaze, so happy to see him, so relieved that he was still here.

"Ro..." he said. Her name reverberated through the room

and Winston glanced down, noticing he still held the microphone to his mouth. Flustered by her presence, he fumbled with it as he put it back in its stand. He cocked his head at her, a puzzled smile on his face, and said, "What are you doing here?" But the swanky background music still pumped through the bar and his words were lost.

Ro couldn't find her voice. The whole bar looked back and forth between her and Winston, waiting for something to happen. Heat rose in her cheeks and she looked at her feet.

Carlos, unable to contain his romantic nature, called out, "She come to stop you, Seńor Winston!"

A group of middle aged men on their way home after vacation, sunburned and half drunk, stood closest to Ro. They watched with amusement.

One of them shouted, "Don't leave her standing there!" They all cheered in agreement.

Ro blushed furiously, uncertain what to do next.

Fortunately, she didn't have to wait long.

Winston hopped off the front of the stage. The crowd parted for him. When she lifted her eyes and saw the look on this face, a shudder went through her body. He watched her evenly as he walked through the crowd, a smile playing on his lips. And something else. Determination.

Winston, her best friend, her confidante, her love, moved towards her so directly, with such intent of purpose, she was helpless in his sights. Her heart pounded in her chest and a tingle moved across her shoulders and up her neck. Her breath came more quickly the closer Winston came, because she knew from the look on his face that he was going to kiss her. As Ro's lips parted ever so slightly in anticipation, Winston reached her.

He placed one hand on her waist, his touch sending a charge of electricity across her skin. Lifting his other hand, he brushed the back of it along her cheek, searching her eyes.

"I got your note," Ro managed to say. Her voice was almost a whisper.

He raised his eyebrows, grinning, "You did?"

She swallowed and nodded, the sensation of his body being just inches away was overwhelming.

"And what did you think?" He asked, letting his eyes wander across her face and lips.

"I wanted to say–" she started.

"Kiss her already!" One of the drunk tourists called out. The rest of the room cheered.

Winston pulled her into him protectively. He held his gaze locked to hers, ignoring the rest of the world. There was nothing but love and desire in his eyes. She wanted to sink into them and stay there forever.

"What did you want to say, Ro?" He asked again.

She ran her hands up his arms and over his shoulders, delighting in the feel of him under her fingertips. Clasping her hands behind his neck, she stood on her tiptoes so he would be sure to hear her over the music and the shouts of encouraging crowd.

"I wanted to say that I love you, Winston."

His arm tightened around her waist as she spoke the words. With great care, he pushed the fingers of his other hand lightly over her ear and into her hair. Ro felt the tension of his body against hers. All of the controlled strength holding her ever so gently made her dizzy with pleasure.

As he bent towards her, his eyes glittering with passion, he whispered, "I love you, too."

And they kissed. With the whooping and hollering of the bar crowd, the happy applause of Carlos and Gloria, and the last notes of the Karaoke song swelling in the air, they kissed.

“Están enamorados!" Carlos shouted, his joy only outdone by their own.

❧

THANK you for reading New Year in Paradise! If you enjoyed this book you may enjoy the other books in the series...

Enchanting Eve - Halloween Romance
Love is at the Table - Thanksgiving Romance
Mistletoe Madness - Christmas Romance

❧

OR YOU MAY ENJOY Darci's Dream Come True series. The first book, Her Scottish Keep is a fun and flirty romance set in the Scottish Highlands...a clean and wholesome contemporary Scottish love story :)

Epilogue

A sweet smelling breeze touched Ro's cheek as she turned to look at the sunrise over the ocean. Her dress lifted and seemed to float as she moved towards the altar. There were no flamingos like in her dreams of Mexico, but the pink in the sky was the same color as those tropical birds. Just like in her dreams, the turquoise water, pristine and clear, shone brilliantly and winked in the morning light.

But this was not a dream.

Her father, dressed in the same sand colored shorts and white gauze shirt as Winston and the groomsmen, looked a little pale and out of place compared to her and Winston, and all of the locals who were present. Still, he was bursting with pride and Ro was thrilled that he and her mother, and the rest of her family, had made it all the way to Playa del Carmen to share in this special day.

Ro's dress had a sleeveless lace bodice and a floor length chiffon skirt, thus the floating on air. They had decided on a beach wedding, of course. Cooper had offered them the use of his yacht, but both she and Winston knew the beach was the right place for them to become man and wife. Just as they'd known that New Year's Day was the right day for them to get married. The yacht would come in handy for their honeymoon weekend, however. They didn't need any more than a long weekend for their honeymoon, because they woke up to paradise every day.

Winston had wasted no time in proposing to Ro after that fateful day in the airport when he'd decided not to get on the plane, but instead drown his sorrows in a cheesy airport bar that happened to offer Karaoke for entertainment. Their love, already settled after knowing one another for so long beforehand, didn't need to be tested out over time for them to know it was true.

Winston had enlisted Carlos' help in helping him plan the proposal. Carlos had suggested taking Ro on a gondola ride through beautiful canals that led to Xcaret park. Winston had popped the question on the gondola and they were met with a romantic dinner for two when they arrived at the park.

Because Carlos played such a big role in their romance, and because he had a huge heart, they had asked him to officiate their wedding ceremony. He had been thrilled at this request and so overcome with emotion Ro had wondered if he would be capable of getting through the wedding without bawling. So far he had been okay, but the day was not yet over.

They had spent the last year getting Winston moved to Playa del Carmen and setting up his business as an accountant to expats living in the area. Ro stayed on at the hotel. How could she leave it after everything Gloria and Carlos, as well as Cooper and Alicia, did to change her life?

She and Winston spent their free time exploring the cenotes and underground rivers in the area. And Zander had taught her how to scuba dive. And, of course, they had been busy with wedding plans, which included this gorgeous beach wedding followed by a reception at the Hotel Diamante.

All of the guests stood as Ro and her father approached. He squeezed her arm and smiled down at her. She gave him a kiss on his cheek, loving him and her mother and this entire day. But most of all, loving Winston.

Winston shook her father's hand and took her arm in his to face Carlos, who was already clearing his throat and fighting back tears. Ro held onto Winston's arm, strong and steady, and thanked her lucky stars that he had come to Mexico to check on her one year ago.

He looked down at her with twinkling eyes, "Ready for this?"

Ro nodded, "I'm ready for all of it."

Winston leaned over and kissed her on the forehead as he covered her hand with his and she lost herself in his warmth and love. A life of adventure was theirs as they became man and wife and the sun rose on a brand new year.

THE FINAL END

Also by Darci Balogh

Want more Sweet Holiday Romance? There are several delightful stories waiting for you....

Sweet Holiday Romance Series (Box Set - great value!)

1. Enchanting Eve

2. Love is at the Table

3. Mistletoe Madness

4. New Year in Paradise (you've got it!)

Dream Come True Series

Five childhood friends vow to live the life of their dreams...without men to mess it all up.

1. Her Scottish Keep

2. Her British Bard

3. Her Sheltered Cove

4. Her Secret Heart

5. Her One and Only

Lady Billionaire Series

1. Ms. Money Bags

2. Ms. Perfect

3. Ms. Know-it-All

Sugar Plum Romance Series

Christmas, cooking, and chefs falling in love!

1. Charlotte's Christmas Charade

2. Bella's Christmas Blunder

Love & Marriage Contemporary Romance (Box Set - best bang for your buck!)

Steamy, emotional stories with relatable characters. These older woman, younger man romances are both racy and romantic.

1. The Quiet of Spring

2. For Love & For Money

3. Stars in the Sand

About the Author

Darci Balogh is a writer and indie filmmaker from Denver. She grew up in the beautiful mountains of Colorado and has lived in several areas of the state over her lifetime. She currently resides in Denver where she raised her two glorious, intelligent daughters to functioning adulthood. This is, by far, one of her highest achievements. She has a love-hate relationship with gardening, probably should dust more, adores dogs and is allergic to cats.

Darci has been a writer since she was a child and enjoys crafting stories into novels and screenplays. Big surprise, some of her favorite pastimes are reading and watching movies. Classic British TV is high on her 'Like' list, along with quietly depressing detective series and coffee with heavy cream.